THE CAPTAIN'S CHEST

BY DONALD WILLERTON

THE CAPTAIN'S CHEST

A MOGI FRANKLIN MYSTERY
BOOK 8

DONALD WILLERTON

WISE WOLF
BOOKS

For My Mother

THE CAPTAIN'S CHEST

CHAPTER 1

JUNE 15, 1718—NORTH OF THE LEEWARD ISLANDS

"It's flying a French flag, sir." Captain Jaan Detrich focused his attention on a ship that had suddenly appeared from behind one of the islands, as if it had been lurking in the shadows, waiting.

"How big, Mr. Fleming?"

"She's bow on, sir, but she's three-masted under full sails. Moving fast, sir," the first mate said.

The captain took the spyglass and studied this new neighbor. Carefully timing the ocean swells as they broke over the bow of the ship in the distance, he judged that his first mate was correct. Moving that fast, it was no merchant ship.

"Add more sail, Mr. Fleming. Then give us thirty degrees to port. We'll see what she does."

The Dutch-owned *Hollander* had taken on a full

belly of cargo in Barbados, with barrels of sugar, rum, and molasses, a hundred bales of cotton, and two hundred smaller bales of silk and calico from India. The remaining space was packed with provisions for the long trip back home to Holland: barrels of water, salt pork and fish, pickled beets, coffee, fruit, chickens, ducks, goats, and other food-stuffs, plus extra sails, rope, and firewood. She was a good ship—a two-masted merchant vessel made for hauling commercial goods between the continents.

She was also a brigantine, carrying long oars for navigating through calm waters, ports, and harbors, and alongside plantation beaches. She had set off from Barbados a week earlier and was now sailing northward in the Caribbean Sea, out of the Leeward Islands and headed to catch the trade winds and eventually the current off the Bahamas that would speed her up the coast of America.

Once past Cape Cod, the captain would turn her east and fly the sheets for home.

She was a good ship, but no fighter. Her crew amounted to twelve sailors, two cabin boys, a cook, a cooper, a carpenter, and three officers.

It wasn't but a few minutes later that Captain Detrich knew the ship on the horizon was, indeed, company he needed to avoid. As his ship changed course and its speed was increased with an added sail, the bigger ship followed, appearing even more intent in its charge toward them.

Apparently the pursuing ship's crew sensed that a chase was beginning, and the French flag was replaced with a long, red streamer snapping smartly in the strong winds above the main sail. The red flag signaled that it was a pirate ship and was now demanding that the *Hollander* heave to and prepare to be boarded.

Looking through his spyglass as the *Hollander* turned, Captain Detrich recognized the carved prow, the decks of cannon ports, and the shape of its sails. He understood who it was he was facing, and it gave him a shiver. He lowered the glass, removed his hat, and gave his forehead a hard swipe. This day would call for sea smarts and courage.

"Mr. Fleming, I believe that Captain Teach intends to pay us a visit."

The first mate's eyes grew wide and he swallowed hard before he spoke.

"Teach, sir? Teach? Good Lord! What shall we do?"

The captain clamped his hat back on his balding head and swept his spyglass across the horizon. He had chosen to sail among the islands of the Drake Channel to put off the harsher weather of the open sea. It was one of the best sailing lanes he knew—deep waters, calm seas, and light winds—and was peppered with many islands should he need shelter or supplies.

His spyglass briefly stopped on the islands of Tortola to his right, St. John to his left, and the Thatch Islands ahead.

He could see dozens of inlets where he might take refuge, but he couldn't be sure of the depth of the water. He needed depth. As much as he could find, as close to the shore as possible.

"Bring up the maps, Mr. Fleming. Let's see where we are. And put us full windward, if you please, with as much cloth as we've got. Make us fast!"

The first mate flew down the stairway, yelling commands that sent the crew scrambling to alter the sails to align with the wind, pushing the speed of the ship for all it was worth. The news of Teach spread like wildfire among the men, and panic set in.

The first mate returned from a cabin below and handed the captain two rolled-up maps. He then returned to watching the sails in the distance.

The captain glanced over the maps, looked at the islands in the distance, counted green bumps, checked the depths of a few coves, used the spyglass, and checked the wind.

"We're going to run for it, Mr. Fleming," he said. "We'll make for the bay east of Mary Point on St. John. We can't win a race on the open sea, but we've a smaller draft. Make it into that bay and they'll think twice about following us in. We'll bury into the beach and make for the forest. Captain Teach, I'm sure, is looking forward to our being his entertainment tonight. He'll want that as much as our cargo, but I do not plan to oblige him."

The smaller ship surged forward under the turning of the sails, curving left, all hands eyeing the land ahead of them and then the ship behind.

Even with full sails, the ship felt like a bobbing log. Every swell seemed to push against her progress, slowing her down and turning her from a clean path. Each seaman worked to eke out every bit of speed he could—tightening a sail, swinging a yardarm in, then out, shifting the square sail off the bow—squeezing power from every breath of the wind.

Having decided his strategy, Captain Detrich now leaned against the ship's rail, appearing cool and calm.

"Steady as she goes, boy," he said to the young man who hung on the rudder arm. "We've got enough of a jump on the ruthless bugger to spoil him in the coral. That point, there—that's Mary Point. Hold that point to star-board. Mr. Fleming!"

The first mate sprinted up from working among the men on the deck below.

"Mr. Fleming, procure my chest and stow the valuables. Pack it well because we'll be slogging her beachside. Ready the long guns and pistols. Make the entry in today's log, then stow the book. Keep the men informed, Mr. Fleming, but we'll buck no slackers today. The iron will be hot on the feet of any who don't make the forest."

The ship in the distance had closed the gap between the two vessels enough that the captain could make out the name carved along the bow: *Queen Anne's Revenge*.

Captured the year before and rebuilt for speed and fighting, she was a thirty-two-gun English warship of massive size. Five decks with a pirate crew of three hundred men, she was known throughout the Caribbean for the ferocious nature of her master: Edward Teach, commonly known as Blackbeard.

A cruel, ruthless animal of a man, Teach was huge —four inches over six feet, almost three hundred pounds—and he ruled his ship and his men with a sadistic glee. He wore an enormous beard, matted and stained with blood, rum, and food, parted and twisted into tails that he decorated with colored ribbons. When he approached his prey for boarding, he sometimes lit long cannon fuses and hung them from under his hat, causing the smoke to surround his face like a grim halo.

To be captured by Blackbeard was to be in the hands of the devil himself. The man enjoyed inflicting pain not only on his enemies, but sometimes even on his friends. Torture was routine, and death the only escape he allowed.

"Swing her around the point!" Captain Detrich yelled as the ship passed by the outlying rocks jutting up through the crashing waves of the island's shore. Every man jumped to the ropes that were tied to the sails. The ship turned quickly, adhering to the line of Mary Point and slipping between coral reefs on each side. Then it rushed into the calm waters of the wide bay, lost its momentum, and stuttered to an almost complete stop. The ocean breezes were now blocked by the tall hills of Mary Point, and the sails went slack.

Immediately, the crew slid long oars through openings in the ship's railings and heaved for the far shore. The captain trotted to the front of the ship, watching the dark shadows of the coral beneath the surface of the water, calling out directions to the boy on the tiller. The more he could thread the ship through the reef, the closer he could get to the beach.

"Pull with all your might, mates—the dogs of hell are descending upon us!"

All the men worked doubly hard, sweat pouring down their faces and blotting their shirts. After only a minute, the ship skidded and balked as its hull scraped against the coral. The men gave all their strength to the final pulls as the ship's keel banged through increasingly shallow water and then slammed into sand fifty feet from the beach. The oars jerked out of their hands and the men spilled onto the deck.

Mr. Fleming instructed the longboat to be lowered. The captain's chest was handed down, the muskets were stowed, and every hand grabbed the smaller boat's oars and shoved them into the water as they jumped to their seats. The captain was last to leave the deck, swinging from a rope to the head of the boat.

The men pulled the oars through the blue and green of the bay and the boat sprinted to the white sand of the beach.

"Ho, seadogs!" the captain yelled at his men. "I know this place. Plantations have been laid out and some roads cut in. Look for paths going up the mountain. The jungle gets thick on both sides, so keep your mind in front of you. We can have no battle here that would not buy us death, so we best run for it. Up the paths, lads, as far as you can, then scatter into the trees. May God be with us this day!

"Mr. Fleming, assign the chest and we'll be on our way."

As Blackbeard surveyed the entrance to the bay, his men gathered the main sails, reducing the ship's speed. He had sailed about the island of St. John before, but his usual anchorage was on the south side, in Rendezvous Bay, where he used the beach for careening his ships. Here on the north side, he was less familiar with the shoreline. He set a man on the prow to sound the depth as he nosed the ship through the bay opening and aimed for the beached brigantine.

When the reef blocked any further progress, he set his anchors, stowed his cannon, and marshaled a boarding party on deck. There was no hurry. He could see a longboat on the beach and watched as a few stragglers disappeared into the forest. He was sure they hadn't set charges in the ship. They would be hoping that their cargo would be enough for him.

And it might be, he thought. He had been headed for the town of Charlotte Amalie on the island of St. Thomas, just north of St. John, for a month's rest and pleasure, so he hadn't needed the extra prize of a Dutch freighter. Raiding over the previous few months had already filled his holds to the limit. However, more cargo meant more money, and the short distance to St. Thomas would allow him to use the crew deck for cargo and to tie bales onto the main deck.

Dividing his crew, he sent most to the *Hollander* for plundering, some into the forest after the escaping crew, and some to scout any settlements along the shore. Since the plantations had not started producing anything yet, there was nothing worth stealing, but there might be *black gold* to be had.

———

Along with four men struggling with the chest, Captain Detrich and Mr. Fleming hurried up a narrow foot-path. Nervously looking over their shoulders to measure their progress from the beach, they watched as the *Queen Anne's Revenge* set her anchors. Seeing the pirates lowering longboats made their feet move faster.

They passed recent diggings and new stonework, outlines of a newly begun sugar mill. Further up the path, they met a dozen slaves. Underfed so severely that their ribs showed, barely clothed and barefoot. At the sight of Detrich and his men, the slaves flung their shovels to the side and disappeared into the jungle. Stolen from their homeland by men who spoke languages they did not understand, they lived in constant terror that they might be, yet again, yanked away and imprisoned on ships in a raging sea, watching their friends die like flies.

Captain Detrich glanced as he hurried by. The slaves were working on an earthen bridge that spanned a large gulley next to the path. The new bridge was probably one of many that would complete the road from the western plantations to St. John's harbor on the east end of the island.

The masonry work of the bridge had been finished. Using a structure of bamboo poles to hold the rock in place until the mortar had set, a curved surface of fitted rock was built to form a wide stone arch from one side of the road to the other. Rock walls were built on the ends of the arch, rising up on each side until the walls extended from one side of the gulley to the other. The space between the walls was filled with sand, broken coral, and rocks from the beach below, brought up one basketful at a time. Smoothing the fill to the road's height with several feet of sand, the slaves had been laying tight-fitting red-colored bricks for the road's surface.

The bricks had been the ballast from the bottom holds of English ships, Captain Detrich thought as he stopped to catch his breath. The plantation owners must have paid a pretty penny for real English bricks.

Ships with tall masts were the best sailing vessels of the day, but they required a large amount of weight in the bottom of each ship to offset the force of the wind on the masts. Without this weight, called *ballast*, ships with tall masts would tip over in strong winds. Usually the ballast material was heavy stones, gravel, or scrap iron from smelters. If so, the ballast was left in place throughout the voyage.

As the building of permanent structures grew in the colonies, smart English merchantmen replaced the regular ballast with tons of heavy clay bricks made in English factories. Tightly packed in the very bottom of the hull, the bricks proved effective as the counterweight necessary to balance the masts.

Fully packed, a merchant ship would set sail from a harbor in England. In Africa, the ship would offload cargo from the upper decks and fill the space with a hundred or more natives captured as slaves, the *black gold* of Africa. Sailing across the Atlantic Ocean to the islands of the Caribbean, the captain would not only sell the remaining cargo and the slaves, but the heavy clay bricks as well, bringing an even greater profit for his entire load.

To replace the weight of the bricks in the bottom of his ship, the captain filled the space with barrels of sugar, rum, and molasses, weighing a thousand pounds each.

They served as ballast on the trip back to England and would be sold on the docks of the Thames. Restoring the ballast with clay bricks would begin another cycle of commerce.

But it was not these thoughts that currently occupied the mind of the *Hollander's* captain. Now hundreds of feet higher than the beach, he finally signaled a stop, his chest heaving as he struggled to catch his breath.

"We've made it about halfway up. Survey a defensive position, Mr. Fleming. I don't expect them up this far, pirates being rather lazy when given a mountain to climb, but we need to lay smart on high ground to give the buggers an uphill battle if needed."

With that, the captain and his men burrowed through the jungle and made secure for a fight.

———

After his men returned empty-handed from chasing the *Hollander* crew up the narrow forest paths, Blackbeard did not pursue his prey any further. His mind had been set on the pleasures of Charlotte Amalie and he was not to be put off any longer.

After a day of pillaging the *Hollander* of its cargo, he swung the *Queen Anne's Revenge* sideways to the abandoned ship and let his crew practice their cannonry.

Within an hour, the poor merchant craft was a bobbing hulk of splintered timbers. Tiring of the game, Blackbeard sent men to set fire to what was left.

It seemed that the *Hollander* gave a last cry as its flaming timbers slowly sizzled into the water.

Captain Edward Teach had his men hook the *Revenge* to the longboats and tow her out of the bay to where she could maneuver on her own. Not looking back, he set sail for the City of Pirates and a retreat of drinking and gambling.

———

Far up the slope of the mountain above the beach, Captain Detrich and Mr. Fleming watched their ship burn.

"Mr. Fleming," the good captain said, "I believe we're on foot from here. We'll make for the settlements, but I would have a barnacle for a brain to think that we should lug the chest with us. Take out our funds and then find a proper place to stow it. I'll go ahead to the beach to assemble the crew, recover anything that might have floated away from the ship, and make plans for the night. Tomorrow, we'll strike for Coral Bay. We'll find another ship and come back for the chest."

It took two days of hard going for the crew to work their way through the forest paths to reach the harbor settlement. Reporting their dire situation to the authorities at Coral Bay, they waited for another Dutch ship to make her regular deliveries before they booked passage back to Barbados. It would be another month before the Captain and his crew procured a new ship and sailed again for Holland.

They should have waited another week.

A few days into their new voyage, the *Hollander's* crew met the *Queen Anne's Revenge* for a second time, but the outcome was not as favorable. Since it was impossible to outrun the bigger ship on the open sea between the islands, Captain Detrich surrendered with few shots fired.

The pirates boarded her, slaughtered the crew, and presented Blackbeard with the captain and his first mate.

The bloodthirsty Teach remembered the encounter from the month before. Complimenting Captain Detrich and Mr. Fleming on their clever escape, he cut off their ears, noses, and lips and hung them by their thumbs, naked in the sun—punishment for spoiling his fun the first time. Their bodies were soon covered in blood, and the birds delighted in picking away their eyeballs, tongues, and other soft tissues. After a few days, once their moans had ceased, Blackbeard cut off their heads and threw the bodies into the sea.

The cabin boys washed the blood from the deck, and Captain Edward Teach continued north to the coastal towns of America.

CHAPTER 2

PRESENT DAY—THE ISLAND OF ST. JOHN, PART OF THE UNITED STATES VIRGIN ISLANDS

Mogi Franklin's throat was dry. He was thirsty like crazy, his stomach was churning—almost cramping—and his eyes were burning from saltwater, sweat, and the sun's glare. Surrounded by an ocean, he thought he should be feeling cool, but the sun reflecting off the water was roasting him like a hotdog.

It was a bad situation, and he didn't know what to do.

He had dreamed of riding a windsurfer so much that he was sure he'd really be good at it. The videos he'd watched made it look like riding a skateboard on steroids, and if you fell off, you hit water, not cement, which sounded like an improvement.

Debating with himself for most of the week, he

finally rented a windsurfer from the Little Maho Bay beachside rental shop and, after two minutes of instruction from the rental guy, launched it from the beach where the water was calm. He stood up, slid his feet into the loops on the board, turned the sail until it caught the breeze, pulled back on the grab bar, picked up speed, and gradually slid across the water.

He'd never felt such raw freedom, and he couldn't help grinning as he flew across the bay. It would have helped if he'd had more weight to pull against the sail, but he was tall, thin, and only fourteen. His gangly arms and legs gave him leverage, but not much power.

Doing turns was the tricky part. Moving from one side of the board to the other, holding on to and adjusting the sail as he walked around it, and then tilting the sail as he took hold of the grab bar on the other side—it was complicated, and he plowed the sail and himself into the water several times. He finally got the hang of it, but preferred just to zoom in one direction and not worry about turning.

Then he came off a swell, made an awkward turn in the air to keep from falling off, and slammed the board flat onto the surface of the water. He heard a loud snap, and the sail yanked him into the air, twisted out of his hands, arced wildly in the wind, and splashed into the water some fifty feet away. Mogi hit the water with a hard slap. Tied to the large board by an ankle tether, he pulled it toward himself, climbed on, and paddled in the direction he guessed the sail had crashed.

He looked around as he rode the waves up and down, but the sail had disappeared.

It was bad enough that the sail had broken, but he realized now that he had no idea where he was. Little Maho Bay was an isolated curve in the shoreline of the much larger Maho Bay, a mile-wide, partly enclosed cove of water on St. John's north side. Wind-surfers were cautioned to stay within the big bay where the ocean currents were mild.

He had not. He had ignored everything except his feeling of freedom and the pure pleasure of zipping across the water. He had zipped straight out of Maho Bay and was a half-mile into the open ocean before he realized the danger. He was making his way back when the sail took off on its own.

Mogi lay on the board, pointed it toward the shore, and used his arms to paddle like he'd seen surfers do on TV.

Despite his efforts, the bay continued to fade into the distance. The current was strong and was moving parallel to the island instead of toward it.

His arms quickly grew tired. He sat up on the board, his legs dangling in the water on each side, looked around at an awfully big, empty sea, and felt a wave of terror. He thought about swimming, but knew he didn't stand a chance—if he couldn't make progress with the board, he'd be doomed without it. Standing up so someone might see him seemed the thing to do, but the heaving of the ocean swells made it impossible. He doubted he could be seen from the shore, anyway.

So he sat. Thinking. Worrying. Burning in the sun. And really needing a drink.

How long could he survive? How long before a ship would pass his way? How fast was he drifting? Would he reach another island? When would Jennifer notice he'd been gone too long? He had told her what he was doing, but would she remember the details? How long before the rental place noticed that he had not returned his windsurfer?

A half-hour later, a large speedboat appeared on the horizon, skimming across the waves toward him. Mogi stood as well as he could and waved his arms frantically.

He was almost in tears as he watched the boat slow and come up beside him.

"Hey, mon, you need a lift?"

The friendly voice was followed by several people reaching over the side of the boat to pull him in. Someone pulled Mogi's windsurfer out of the water and tied it to the deck. The people on board—a group of tourists and two islanders—all introduced themselves, but Mogi was not yet able to speak.

As the boat accelerated in a curve and headed toward the land in the distance, Mogi struggled to stop his shaking.

Someone offered him a bottle of water and he guzzled it without shame, so very thankful for the taste of fresh water.

"He saw you when he was up in de air, mon," a tall islander in shorts and a T-shirt explained, pointing to one of the passengers. The islander had a lyrical accent, pronouncing several words differently from what Mogi was used to, such as *mon* for *man* and *de* instead of *the*.

The boat was equipped for parasailing, with a large metal pipe arching from side to side and a broad platform at the rear. The two islanders were in the business of belting their passengers into a harness hooked to a parachute.

When the boat accelerated, the parachute, attached by a cable to a winch, filled with air and lifted the passenger high into the sky. From all accounts, the ride was beyond thrilling.

A few minutes later, they pulled up to the beach in Little Maho Bay and returned Mogi and his broken windsurfer to the shore. Laughing and waving, the parasailers took off, carving a huge wave with the bow as they went back out into the ocean.

With his feet on the sand, with the entire Earth solidly below him, Mogi finally closed his eyes and let the relief sweep over him.

————

"Uh, so what about the sail?" he said to the rental guy. "Am I going to have to pay for it or something?"

"Nah. I'm sorry it broke. That's really unusual. We'll send somebody out with a jet ski to look for it, but I doubt they'll find it. It'll wash up on shore somewhere, and we'll eventually get it back. I'll give you your rental fee back since it was an equipment failure."

Mogi gave another deep sigh of relief—wind-surfers cost over two thousand dollars. Not being responsible for the broken sail made things a lot better.

He thanked the man, bought another bottle of water, and started hiking up to the resort, leaving the clean, fresh air of the shoreline and plunging into the wet, thick air of the jungle.

Some hundred yards up the walkway, Jennifer's cottage was more of a tent than a building. The top and sides were made of canvas and screen, but the canvas was stretched over a wooden frame that formed it into a small, semi-permanent, cabin-like structure. The hard door and zip-up screens let in the much-appreciated breeze but kept the birds, bats, iguanas, mongooses, snakes, and creepy-crawlies on the outside.

In Mogi's mind, it was the perfect escape from the harsh sun and the circling insects.

There were over a hundred cottages perched on wooden platforms, built on posts high above the jungle floor. The tropical forest surrounded the plat-forms with drooping coconut palms and the heavily leafed branches of other trees. Built atop the giant ferns, tall grasses, and creeping vines on the ground, the cottages were mostly hidden behind huge curtains of green, with an occasional splash of bright yellow and orange flowers.

The cottages were connected to each other and to the resort's facilities by wooden walkways that threaded through the forest in a dozen directions.

The walkways led up and down the steep slopes of the mountainous terrain, beginning and ending at the resort's office building and restaurant. They were located halfway up the mountain at the end of a paved road.

Altogether, the walkways, cottages, and buildings made up the Maho Bay Beachcomber Resort, one of only a few privately owned vacation resorts hugging the north shore of the island of St. John, the second largest island in the U.S. Virgin Islands, and part of the more than a thousand islands known as *the Caribbean*.

The office building and restaurant were the center of activity for the resort's business. Mogi's sister, Jennifer, who was seventeen, worked in one of the craft buildings as a recycler, helping to convert the worn sheets and linens of the resort into shirts, pants, napkins, placemats, comforters, quilts, and other items that were sold in the gift shop and in the village of Cruz Bay, St. John's largest town. Cruz Bay was on the western tip of the island, a thirty-minute ride by the resort's shuttle or by the island's minibus, which could be boarded at the public parking lot near the beach.

Winded from sprinting up the walkways, Mogi collapsed at a shaded table outside the restaurant and used a fistful of napkins to mop the sweat pouring down his face.

The heat wasn't the problem. In his hometown of Bluff, Utah, it was typically hotter, with the temperature hovering around a hundred degrees in the summer. But the air was dry there, and the vegetation amounted to scattered clumps of grass, tamarisk trees along the San Juan River, a handful of juniper and piñon trees, and isolated cottonwoods, all of which had a tiny effect on the miles of barren slickrock sandstone that dominated the landscape. It was the opposite of a jungle, and the humidity was commonly in the single digits.

St. John, however, even with temperatures in the eighties and nineties, was surrounded by ocean and covered in dense jungle. The thick vegetation held the moisture close to the ground, filling the air with water vapor that made Mogi sweat continuously. In Utah, his sweat evaporated almost immediately. Here, it ran in continuous streams. If he didn't keep drinking water, he'd shrivel like a raisin.

Living on an island in the Caribbean was as far out of his experience as living on the moon.

CHAPTER 3

The restaurant's television was on. As he flopped back in the chair, Mogi could not take his eyes off the program. There were no other TVs at the resort, nor any cellphone service. He hadn't seen any TV for more than a week and couldn't help but be hypnotized.

Great, he thought as the weatherman walked in front of a full-screen map of the Atlantic. My first time here and there's a hurricane coming. A weird, early-season hurricane that no one even understands.

The restaurant's usual dinner crowd began wandering in. Mogi waved to Jennifer as she approached. She was shorter than him by a few inches, athletic and graceful, and had thick brown hair, cut short. Whenever their dad told her she was cute as a bug, Mogi always had to suggest exactly which bug she was being compared to.

"Do you know there's a hurricane coming?" he asked as she sat down.

"Oh, yeah, but it's still a thousand miles out at sea or something. Everybody says it'll miss us. We'll maybe get a little rain later this week, but I'm not worried about it."

"We ought to get our snorkeling in soon, just in case. A hurricane could really mess up the water, especially such a weird, early one."

Jennifer looked closely at Mogi and then touched his red face. "Good grief! You're burnt to a crisp! Did you fall asleep on the beach or something?"

He told her of the afternoon's adventure, what it was like to be stuck out in the middle of the ocean, and how he was rescued by the parasailing crew. Jennifer listened politely. Then she ripped him from top to bottom about being stupid and careless. He might get away with mistakes hiking in the back-country of Utah, but the ocean was far less forgiving! She made him promise to be more careful.

"You're supposed to be studying, anyway. That was the only way Mom and Dad let you come visit for a month, remember?"

"Yeah, yeah, yeah, I'll do it. I promise. Seriously, I will learn the history of the Caribbean and the people and everything. It's just my first week, so you have to give me a break for being a little overwhelmed with the place. And I do appreciate you putting up with me, honest."

Jennifer was a summer volunteer at the resort. In exchange for nearly three months of labor, she was given a cottage of her own and substantial discounts at the resort's restaurant, rental shop, gift shop, and small market. The job was only on weekdays, from 9 a.m. to 2 p.m., leaving her afternoons and weekends free to explore both the U.S. and British Virgin Islands. Even though the arrangement was costing her money rather than making it, their parents thought that experiencing the islands and its culture was an opportunity she shouldn't miss.

Then, of course, Mogi begged to visit. Volunteers were allowed to have guests stay in the cottages for free, so there was no additional cost for housing, but he had to pay for his own food. Since he would only be there for July, she didn't mind saving him from the mind-numbing summer jobs in Bluff. But she was happy that he wasn't going to get it without working for it.

"We're both lucky," she said. "If my friend Sue hadn't been here last year and told me about it, I'd probably be back cashiering at the gas station all summer. But I'm working, and I'm not about to nursemaid you. You are totally responsible for upholding your end of the bargain. I wouldn't be surprised if Mom doesn't make you write a paper when you get back home. Or make you give a slideshow."

Mogi laughed, even though he knew she might not be far from wrong. He had promised that he would learn about the history of the Caribbean, the islands' culture, and the relationship of the islands to the history of America. And he *was* interested in all of it, especially stories about pirates.

Mogi took after his mom's side of the family in his

looks and his shyness, but seemed to be a sum of both families on the brain side: He was way smarter than most of the people around him. Quick-minded, mentally disciplined, and methodical, he had a natural talent for solving puzzles. That made visiting a different country a challenging adventure on all sorts of levels, and he wasn't about to blow it.

"I am absolutely going to do what I promised. I had planned on reading a few books, but talking with the guy who runs the St. Thomas Maritime Museum in Charlotte Amalie is going to make everything easier and far more interesting. You met Griffin Powers when we stopped there on our first day, remember? I told him how you were volunteering here and how I was tagging along for a month.

"Well, he picked up a pencil and outlined the history of the Caribbean on a single piece of paper. He offered to talk me through it whenever I wanted. I've already been over there two mornings this week —the ferry to and from St. Thomas is quick and cheap.

"You wouldn't believe how much this guy knows. And he loves to talk—boy, does he love to talk. I must be saving him from being bored. He even gives me assignments. And if that wasn't enough, I've got the park's visitor center and the historical museum in Cruz Bay. They've got tons of exhibits, maps, books, and history brochures, plus self-guided tours to all the ruins on the island.

"Which reminds me—one of the park rangers is willing to give us a tour of the island, and he'll throw in a history lecture for free. He offered to do it this Saturday, if you're interested."

"Sounds good to me," she replied. "Are we still going diving tomorrow afternoon?"

"You bet. I reserved the tanks, masks, fins, and other stuff this morning. Everything will be ready when you get off work. One of the resort people will run us down to Leinster Bay, which is only a half-mile away, and come back for us about five. That gives us time after we dive to look for treasure."

"Treasure? There's treasure?"

"A genuine buried treasure chest full of jewels and gold. All we have to do is find it."

"So, it's taken you only a week to find us another hair-brained adventure?" Jennifer asked. "You're usually faster than that."

Mogi smiled. He seemed to have a talent for finding adventures, usually linked to some mystery or legend or riddle and, unfortunately, he had put both himself and his sister in some dangerous situations as a result.

"Well," he said, "I don't think there's much chance of finding this particular treasure chest. It's a great story, though. It was buried about three hundred years ago by some ship escaping from Blackbeard the pirate.

"But I promise I'm not going to get mixed up in any mysteries or anything. Everything this month is just going to be for fun."

Jennifer rolled her eyes. "Oh, sure," she said. "I've heard that before."

CHAPTER 4

Mogi and Jennifer pulled the dive equipment from the back of the resort's golf cart, thanked the driver, and looked around to get their bearings. Leinster Bay was roughly rectangular, open to the sea along the north side with the peninsula of Mary Point to the left and a curving finger of land called Leinster Point far away on the right. In between, a mile or so of white sand beach rimmed a vast pool of clear blue ocean. Next to the road, a small sign pointed toward the bay where the water now cloaked the ancient shipwreck of the *Hollander*.

Mogi read the information card given to him by the rental shop manager:

"It was in 1718 when Blackbeard the pirate chased a Dutch trading ship named the *Hollander*, intending to capture it and steal its cargo. Outrunning Blackbeard to this bay, the captain and the crew rammed their ship onto a sandbar near the beach and escaped into the forest. When Blackbeard found the abandoned ship, he emptied it of cargo and set it on fire. If you swim directly out from the *Hollander Shipwreck* sign, you will see the remaining pieces of the masts and the hull. Since the back end of the ship was in deeper water and burned less, the sides become more prominent farther from the shore."

After running through their equipment check and pulling on their tanks, Jennifer goose-stepped after her brother, her fins making comical prints in the sand. The water swept up around them as they walked awkwardly through the shallows to deeper water. Finally, almost floating, they put their heads into the water, tested their goggles and respirators, lifted their legs, and let the weight of their equipment take them below the surface.

Life changed instantly.

The strong sun, the rhythmic sounds of the surf, and the pull of gravity were replaced by a veil of shadowy light, a silence broken only by the bubbling of their respirators, and the freedom of near weightlessness. The two drifted with the rhythm of the waves, shifting and tightening their tanks, knives, belts, safety vests, and other equipment. Satisfied, the siblings powered their fins and dropped into the sea life below them, each releasing a stream of bubbles as they descended.

Big clumps of coral lay scattered across the floor of the bay, with crooked avenues of clear sand winding among them. It took careful maneuvering to avoid the hard, unimaginably rough clumps of coral, but soon, they passed over the tops of the clumps and dove deeper.

Mogi arched his body and leveled out just above the sea floor, snaking his way up, over, and around the ruggedness of the bottom. The light from above was in constant motion, shimmering against the varying greens and browns below. He avoided the spiny sea urchins that blossomed in reds and purples but watched as schools of brightly colored fish darted in and out of the pockmarked surface of the coral. Looking ahead, he spotted a series of regular shapes.

He and Jennifer swam past an uplifted rock and found themselves swimming down the spine of a colonial-era cargo vessel. The massive oak beams that were the ship's ribs curved up and out of the sea floor on each side of them, covered with saltwater plants and thick crusts of algae. A couple of tall columns might have been the remainders of the masts.

An amazing array of fish darted around Jennifer as she held out her hand. Small and smaller, there were yellows, blacks, oranges, bright blues, greens, reds, dots, stripes, and shimmering smears of color—a complete color palette as if laid on with the brilliant strokes of a brush. The fish swam singly or in schools of several dozen.

Against the electric color of the fish, the coral lay with unmoving bulk, more uniform within the ship-wreck than around it, varying from whites and tans to pale greens and dark greens to dark browns and blacks, looking sometimes like broccoli, sometimes like rounded lumps of brain, and sometimes like gentle fans. Many were adorned with long, stringy plants swaying in the water like lightly colored beards.

Jennifer pointed as a sea turtle swam past her and was stunned as several jellyfish floated by, making their graceful dancing moves as their ghostly skins contracted and expanded.

Mogi prowled along the distorted humps of coral between the ship's ribs and looked closely at the camouflaged beams. Even though the wreck was covered with growth, he could sense its size and structure. He considered the number of barrels of molasses and sugar that must have filled its interior, how fat and heavy the ship must have been when fully loaded, how confined its spaces must have felt during the long voyages across the sea. Sailors were hardy men, he thought. They had to be incredibly tough to face those long months of harsh conditions.

Swimming past the rear of the ship and above the wreck by ten or twenty feet, the Franklins were better able to see the outline of the hull. Though it was covered with a thick crust, it still appeared on the ocean floor as a ship—abandoned, and perhaps even haunted by its violent end.

Satisfied with their discovery, they descended again and prowled along the edge of the reef, watching the darting fish, the scurrying lobsters, the gliding black manta rays, and taking in the general beauty of ocean life. They carefully watched as a large barracuda swam lazily through a patch of green sea grass waving in the current.

After they got out of the water and dried off, they dragged their equipment through the sand and up to the road, where someone from the Beachcomber would pick them up.

Mogi gazed thoughtfully toward the ship and wondered if, in all that mess, anyone could really think about hauling a chest up such a steep slope.

"What are you thinking?" Jennifer asked.

"It must have been pretty freaky to be chased by Blackbeard. You've got a crew of what, a dozen? Being chased by a warship with hundreds of pirates? They must have lost their lunch! I wonder if we could figure out where they actually went."

"Sure," Jennifer replied. "Why not? It's only been three hundred years. Maybe we can look for their footprints."

"Well," Mogi said with a shrug. "You never know."

CHAPTER 5

As they approached the slope, Jennifer pointed upward and asked, "So, the treasure chest is up that hill somewhere?"

"It could be anywhere between the beach and the top of the mountain," Mogi answered. "Griffin Powers talked about it this morning.

"The ship was rammed into the sand, and the captain and his men went overboard into a rowboat with all the valuables in the captain's chest. They lugged the chest up the hill, hoping the pirates wouldn't chase them and expecting to return to the ship after Blackbeard had plundered it. But when he set it on fire, the captain and his crew were stranded. They had to walk to the east end of the island, where the harbor was. Not wanting to carry the chest, they hid it somewhere before they left, planning on returning for it when they got another ship.

"When the captain and his crew got to the harbor in Coral Bay, they told the authorities of the attack on the *Hollander*. Then, hitching a ride to Barbados, a major shipping hub at the time, the Dutch shipping company provided them with a new ship. They were on their way back to retrieve the chest when they were again chased by Blackbeard. He caught them in the open sea, forced them to surrender, and then chopped the heads off of everybody on board.

"The people in Coral Bay knew that the captain had hidden the ship's chest after the first attack, but he hadn't told anyone the location. Since everybody was killed in the second attack, it was lost forever."

"Well, that's not fair," Jennifer said. "Don't they normally leave a map with a big *X* on it?"

Mogi laughed. "Only in *Treasure Island.* Griffin says the locals probably dug up every square inch of the island but never found it."

The teens spent the next hour walking through the ruins of various plantations around the bay—the storage houses, the tall walls of the windmill where the sugar cane was crushed, the factory building where the cane juice was strained and heated, and the stone cooling tanks where the concentrated juice, by then called molasses, evaporated into the rough brown crystals of sugar.

According to the guidebook, the Annaberg School, a hundred yards up the beach from where the *Hollander* wreck lay beneath the waves, served both free and slave children beginning in 1839. Across from the school's ruins was a preserved section of the original Danish Road, built in the early 1700s, even before the plantations were operating. The section of the road now appeared only as a dip in the landscape, but ran from the beach through a flat area of low bushes and then up into the dense foliage of the hill-side. With a paved park-service road running next to it, the old path appeared every now and then as a worn path in the forest.

Plodding up the paved road to get a greater view of the bay, Mogi and Jennifer stopped to catch their breath as the road curved to the right, cutting across the steepness of the mountainside. They stood for a moment, admiring the paradise of the peaceful bay and the white seabirds swooping through the sky.

"Look at that," Jennifer said, pointing off the road.

An old stone bridge peeked out of the jungle. Made of native rocks set in mortar, a low, graceful arch of fitted stones rose out of the jungle floor, span-ning a gulley about twenty feet wide. It looked to be about ten feet above a well-washed, dry streamed of sand and rock and pebbles.

Mogi left the blacktop of the modern road and walked across the flat roadway still supported by the bridge, stepping on a cushioned layer of leaves, vines, grasses, and black soil. "This must have been the road put in by the original plantation owners," he said. "The guidebook says it ran from the Coral Bay harbor all along the coast up here, connecting the plantations together."

Jennifer followed her brother onto the bridge. "This thing feels massive and amazingly flat," she said. She knelt on the littered surface. Digging away hand-fuls of fresh leaves, rotted leaves, and a thick layer of loam and black dirt, she wiped enough of the covering away to reveal a pattern of dark edges.

"Look at this," she said.

Mogi knelt beside her and scraped back more of the covering. Underneath was a uniform layer of hard brick.

"Wow," he said. "This might be the original surface of the roadway. It looks like paving brick, which means that this was a pretty serious road."

He tried to imagine making a road through the rugged landscape with only primitive tools like shovels and picks.

Doing it once would have been hard enough, but he guessed there were dozens of gullies that carried rainfall from the tops of the mountains. Each one of them would have been a threat to wash away the road and would have required a bridge.

No bulldozers, backhoes, dump trucks, or road graders.

They did it all by hand, every time, for every gulley.

He rose, walked around the bridge, dropped down into the streambed below, and walked underneath the stonework.

"Come look at this!" he called to his sister, running his hand up against the graceful arch of stone. "It's masonry that's lasted three hundred years. The gulley has never filled in, no doubt being wiped clean every time a heavy rain poured down it. Let's see if there's a cornerstone."

Mogi looked at the stones at the bottom of the

arch, knelt, and pulled handfuls of sand, rock, pebbles, grass, weeds, and vines away from the bottom of the archway.

"There we go," he said.

Jennifer looked at the rough stone her brother had uncovered. On the surface, the date *1718* had been chiseled deeply into a large rock that had served as the anchor stone for the bridge.

"Wow," Mogi said as he squatted and brushed more dirt from the engraving. "It was built the same year that Blackbeard chased the *Hollander*. This stone may have been here when the ship was burning in the bay."

They picked their way through the vegetation and returned to the blacktop just in time to hear a ship's horn in the distance. Looking toward the entrance to the bay below them, an extraordinary ship had anchored just inside. It was an enormous yacht with a long, sweeping, artistically crafted hull, shaped like a dolphin and painted a shiny gunmetal gray. There were no individual windows to be seen, just continuous black panels of glass that stretched the length of each of several levels while the top was covered with a half-dozen or more tall antennae next to two large, white, radar domes. The sleek windows of the pilot-house were contoured to slice through a rushing wind, more like a plane than a ship.

"Wow," was all Mogi could say.

Several jet skis zoomed in and around the bay's entrance, with people laughing and shouting, racing each other, making tight turns that lifted sprays of water high into the air. A platform from the back of the boat had been extended to make a just-above-the-water deck, where chairs and tables and umbrellas had been placed.

Through his binoculars, Mogi watched as they dove and swam around the platform, the people all athletic and beautiful and excited and social, acting as if there were nothing to do in the world except have fun.

Wish that was me, Mogi thought.

CHAPTER 6

"Glen Parry," the uniformed man said as he extended a friendly handshake.

"Hi, I'm Jennifer."

"Are you ready for a tour?"

Saturday was like the other days Mogi had spent on the island—bright, clear, hot, a constant breeze coming off the ocean, and the air scented everywhere with vibrant plant life. Everyone except the true islanders sported sweat-stained clothes and carried handkerchiefs or towels to wipe their faces. Being in the shade was better, but just barely.

Mogi swung his daypack in front of him and jumped into the back seat of the Jeep. As soon as Jennifer was settled in the front seat, Ranger Parry eased the Wrangler down the road to the bay, turned right at the Annaberg School intersection, and soon passed the jungle-hidden stone bridge they had seen the day before. Farther up the hill, a left turn put them on the main highway of the island, Centerline Road.

"Two-thirds of the island of St. John is the Virgin Islands National Park," Ranger Parry said. "It sits between the town of Cruz Bay on the west end and the smaller town of Coral Bay on the east end. The park gets more than a million visitors a year, so it's the major industry of the island.

"Today we're going to East End, which is the far side of the biggest bay on the island, also called Coral Bay. It's not part of the park. I'll point out a few beaches and snorkeling spots along the way, if you're interested. The whole island is only nine miles long and five miles wide. It's the very top of an old volcanic mountain, which makes driving a challenge because of the ups and downs of the terrain."

Centerline Road was paved and in good shape, but the road confirmed what the ranger had said. The Jeep's passengers were jostled in their seats as the road coursed through steep-sided gullies, down and up small valleys, and then along the ridges of the hills. The Jeep's suspension system did little to cushion the jolts and swerves.

The road finally descended from the rough terrain.

Dominating the view to the right, Coral Bay was large, maybe two miles in width and length, with the inlet to the ocean in the distance across from them. Wide and with good depth, plenty of flat beach, and protection from the open ocean, the large bay had served as the historical port for trading ships, military cruisers, and personal sailboats. The town supporting the port activities had been St. John's largest town until a ferry service was begun from St. Thomas to Cruz Bay, on the other end of the island. Afterward, tourism became the primary source of income, and the town of Coral Bay shrank to just a village.

"This is the very eastern part of the island," Ranger Parry said. "We're passing through the upper tip of the Coral Bay township. Ahead is a narrow part of the land that curves down the side of the bay, called East End.

Local people owned this part of the island until about two years ago when a billionaire named Oscar Padilla bought the southernmost piece. Except for a small stretch of connecting land, the Padilla property is almost a little island of its own. Mr. Padilla plans on building a theme park on the property."

"He wants to build a theme park?" Jennifer exclaimed. "You mean like Disneyland or something? You've got to be kidding. Who's going to go to it?"

"Well, he wants cruise ships to pull in here, like they do in St. Thomas. Thousands of people would get off and play for the day, then load back up and pull out before sunset. The park wouldn't even have a hotel. He could possibly have five thousand people here at any one time, so it has the potential to make a lot of money."

Mogi whistled. "It's hard to imagine that St. John could support something like that. Where would he get the workers?"

"Not from St. John, obviously. There're only four thousand people who live on St. John itself, and most are already employed in one way or another. Padilla would need hundreds on a daily basis. I think he's counting on people coming from other islands around here, plus college students from all across America who would work part-time during the year."

"Are islanders in favor of this?" Jennifer asked.

"Not even close. It might mean more jobs and more income, but a big attraction always hurts local businesses, and that's basically all there is on the island. Besides, the new jobs aren't the kind of jobs people want. We'd just end up with a bunch of under-paid people who would be as much a burden on the island as an improvement.

"The theme park would need a lot of electricity, generate tons of trash and sewage, and require tremendous amounts of freshwater. Padilla appar-ently believes he can solve those problems, but I think he's fooling himself."

"What would the theme of the park be?" Mogi asked.

"He plans to call it *Blackbeard's Island*, complete with pirate ship rides, hunting for buried treasure, roller coasters, gondola rides, and daily sea battles between the pirates and the good guys."

Ranger Parry pulled to a quick stop in front of a heavily barred gate and fence across the road.

"This is the entrance to Padilla's land. Everything on the other side is where the theme park would be. I wanted to check if the gate was still shut and see if anything had changed since the last time I was here. Now we'll go back to the village and go south until the road ends. In Coral Bay, I have someone I want you to meet."

————

Entering Coral Bay was not what Mogi had expected.

The town of Cruz Bay on the other end of the island, where he caught the daily ferry to St. Thomas, fit within a small, curved shoreline surrounded by hills. It had paved streets, shops, hotels, restaurants, food stands, a harbor full of small boats, streets with lights, and other features typical of a town that served tourists.

The village of Coral Bay was spread out and far more rustic: White-plastered huts were scattered among the palm trees and bushes, and businesses lined the highway instead of the streets. Few street-lights, no hotels, no restaurants, and hardly any shops. The waters of the bay were calm and clear with dark splotches of coral reefs, white-sand beaches, and colorful sailboats anchored, gently swaying back and forth.

It certainly lacked the hustle and bustle of the traffic and tourists in Cruz Bay. Looking across the bay to the east, Mogi saw the forested shores and hills of the lower part of East End, which was, he guessed, all Padilla property. He couldn't imagine cruise ships emptying thousands of people onto the beaches just to play pirate.

Ranger Parry pulled the Wrangler up a sandy lane and stopped in front of a large, white-plastered house.

Through the front door stepped a tall, handsome, well-built islander wearing shorts, sandals, and a Miami Heat T-shirt.

Mogi recognized him immediately.

"Adam!" Ranger Parry called. The islander responded with a wide smile. When he reached the Jeep, he extended a big hand to Mogi. "Hey, mon, you need a lift?"

They both laughed. Adam was the pilot of the parasailing boat that had rescued the poor Utah boy from the grips of the wide ocean.

"This is Adam Deschamp," Ranger Parry said as Adam climbed in the back beside Mogi. "He was born here. His family is one of the original families of St. John, one of the few that still retain the ownership of their land."

"You ever want to dive for conch," Adam said with a wink, "I'm your mon."

"He went to Texas A&M for college and now owns a parasailing business that operates all around the islands," Ranger Parry continued.

"He's also pretty good in the rescue business," Mogi added and went on to tell of his experience with the windsurfer, again recognizing how fortunate he had been that Adam came along.

A mile and a half down the road, Ranger Parry pulled the Jeep into an overlook on top of a small hill. As everyone got out, he pulled out a pair of binoculars, leaned on the hood, and scouted the distant shape of East End.

Adam stood beside him as they exchanged information on what had been happening in the bay and whether any ships had anchored off the far shore.

"Something wrong?" Mogi asked, not understanding the conversation.

"I hope not," Ranger Parry said. "I'm not the suspicious type, but I think Mr. Padilla hasn't been telling us the whole truth."

"We don't trust de mon," Adam said, his Caribbean accent adding a musical beat to his deep voice. "I've asked Adam to keep watch on East End. Unfortunately, Padilla's facilities are on the other side, so there's not much to see from here. They have a harbor in a small bay just on the other side of that hill, which, I assume, is used to offload equipment and people. I'd still expect to see some activity on this side, though. Right now, there doesn't seem to be anything at all happening, and that puzzles me."

"What are you expecting? Wouldn't people be happier if he took a long time to build his theme park?" Jennifer asked.

"Taking a long time to build means more time putting up with a construction mess. If it's going to happen, most people would prefer to get it over with. It's taken about two years for him to make all the right arguments about the electricity, the water, and the waste. Now Padilla is waiting on the approvals to remove some of the coral reefs around East End so he can build a long dock where cruise ships can park to offload people. Just that part of his operation could take years."

"I thought offshore coral reefs were protected," Mogi said.

"That's true for most of the island, but not off the shore of Padilla's property. If he gets the approvals, he'll dredge his side of the bay to get the water depth needed for the dock."

"That's a terrible thing to do!" Jennifer said. "It'll ruin everything beautiful about this place. How can he get away with it?"

"De mon has money," Adam said. "Congress likes a mon with money. And jobs. Everybody likes it when you talk jobs."

Coming around the west tip of Coral Bay and moving across the bay's opening, a large boat came into view.

Mogi could see that it was twin-hulled, like a catamaran, with two stories above the deck, gleaming white, and around sixty feet long. The pilot's cabin was fully wrapped with dark glass. Several antennae waved above the top.

"Wow, that's a nice boat," he said.

"That's Padilla's supply boat," Ranger Parry said. "It runs over to St. Thomas every day. Sometimes twice. It picks up groceries, water, mail, then comes back. When I've been in St. Thomas at the same time, I've rarely seen anybody on it other than a couple of crew members and the cook."

"Okay, so back to my question," Jennifer said, curious now about what Ranger Parry had been saying. "What would you expect to see if everything was okay?"

Ranger Parry stood up, resting the binoculars on the Jeep. "Little red flags. There should be hundreds of little red construction flags. You know those little red flags about two feet tall that you see when a trench is going to be dug, or a line buried, or an irrigation line is being laid out? To figure out how the theme park would fit on his land, there should be lots of workers with measuring tapes—laying out walkways, benches, shade trees, park rides, restaurants, buildings, water lines, electrical lines, waste lines, everything that a construction project would need. Even if Padilla doesn't do anything until the paperwork has been approved, he should still be planning. I would expect little red flags all over the place.

"I don't see any flags at all. Not a one. It's like the land hasn't even been surveyed. Most of Padilla's time during the last two years has been in the courts, arguing over utilities, but it looks like nothing at all has been done to lay out the theme park. To me, that's odd."

Ranger Parry stood, ran his eyes over the distant shore, and looked grim.

"Between me and you, I don't think he's planning on building anything. I think he bought it as an investment. He's out to show that Congress can be bought, that the island government will roll over and that the locals will follow like sheep. When it all comes through, he'll sell that land for ten times what he paid for it and let someone else do the building."

"He's exploiting the island," Jennifer said. "He's exploiting the island, the people, the land, the ocean, and everything that's beautiful about it so he can make more money. I don't like this guy."

Mogi watched the supply boat pass by the tip of East End, disappearing around the corner, no doubt into Padilla's hidden bay. He couldn't understand building a park here. There weren't even regular streetlights in Coral Bay. This random billionaire would take everything the place was and replace it with everything it wasn't. It would be like an invasion of an alien species.

He watched a sailboat run up its sails and slip out of the bay. It turned, ran up a larger sail to gain speed, and was soon zipping across the waves. The ocean was so vast and the island so small. Why pick this place?

To the east, above the hills, he noticed that the sky was dark close to the horizon.

"Is that the hurricane in the distance?" Mogi asked.

"The hurricane is several hundred miles wide, so what you see is the fringe of the clouds," Ranger Parry said.

"I'm not worried much about it, but it is coming toward us more than we originally thought. We've got evacuation plans if something bad happens, but we're keeping an eye on this storm. If it doesn't change direction pretty soon, we could be in big trouble."

CHAPTER 7

On Monday, Mogi was back on St. Thomas for another history lesson.

"You didn't see the *Hollander's* anchor?"

"Oh, man! There was an anchor?" Mogi whined. "Mr. Powers, no one told me there was an anchor. I would have loved to have seen that!"

The burly man laughed. "First, call me Griffin. Second, well, now you know. You can go back and have something to look for."

Griffin Powers was the manager of the Maritime Museum of Charlotte Amalie, the largest city on the island and a forty-five-minute ferry ride from St. John. It was Griffin who had offered to teach Mogi the history of the Caribbean.

"I've been everywhere and done everything," he had said when he first introduced himself. "I was a ground-pounder in Vietnam and a wanderer afterward. At some point, I'd had enough of Southeast Asia and wanted to see more of the world. I couldn't speak anything but English, so I crewed on a rich guy's sail-boat while he shuttled around the Pacific islands. He turned out to be a jerk, so I jumped ship in Tahiti, knocked around for a while, and ended up here in the eighties.

"I've worked on a wharf cutting up fish, served as a cook on sailboat charters going up and down the islands, worked on the ferry for almost ten years, taught high school, and helped clean up some of the plantation ruins on St. John. I fancied myself a writer for a while, writing travel articles about the Caribbean, Mexico, and Central America, and even got shot at by Colombian drug lords because of some-thing I wrote about their business that they didn't want people to know.

"When my sea legs wore out, I finally got a desk job, and here I am, a fount of wisdom and informa-tion and hardly anybody to talk to."

Mogi had liked him right away.

"You been around St. John much yet?" Griffin asked.

Mogi told him about the afternoon he and Jennifer had spent with Ranger Parry and Adam, driving to the end of the Coral Bay highway where Ranger Parry pointed out the various beaches along the coast, told stories of who had done what, and pointed out the good snorkeling spots close to Coral Bay. On the way back, they dropped Adam at his house and then returned to Centerline Road. As a special treat, he turned off on the Bordeaux Mountain Road and took them up a steep incline to the highest point of the island.

"Most of the coastline below us," Ranger Parry said as he pointed his finger across the island's south shore, "can only be gotten to by trails through the forest or by boats from the water. It's kind of a shame, but it certainly keeps the countryside free of litter. You two need to rent a boat for a day or go with a tour group from town that takes you around the island. There's some really good snorkeling and diving to be had, that's for sure."

The end of the tour took them to Gift Hill Road. It ran through the more populated areas of the island, with overlooks, small villages, houses, and a few hotels, and eventually led them into the downtown area of Cruz Bay.

The Franklins ate dinner at a sandwich shop and then caught the island bus back to the resort in time for the Saturday night movie at the restaurant. Sunday was spent walking around Maho Bay and playing volleyball on the beach below the Beachcomber.

"So you got a look at Rendezvous Bay, did ya?" Griffin asked.

Mogi thought for a minute. "I remember it being mentioned. Was that the big bay below Gift Hill?"

"I'm impressed you remembered. It was a famous gathering place for pirates."

"Pirates?"

"Yep. Of course, there were pirates all over the islands, but Rendezvous Bay was a favorite place. It has a stretch of good beach with no coral. Pirates used it to career their ships. You know what *careening* means?"

"Uh, no."

"Whenever a ship has been at sea for a long time, especially if it's a wooden ship, stuff grows on its hull, like algae, barnacles, and such. That makes it slow in the water, which pirates hate because you can't catch up with ships that you want to rob, and you can't outrun your enemies. So every six months or so, they'd need to scrape all that yuck off the bottom of the ship. That's what *careening* a hull means.

"You sail your ship into a bay with shallow water and lots of coral-free beach, like Rendezvous Bay. Then you run it up on the beach at high tide as far as you can and set the anchor. When the tide goes out, the boat stays on the beach and exposes the bottom of the boat. The crew gets out there with knives, chisels, hammers, and whatever, and they clean all the bad stuff off. They may also fix anything broken on the ship, like damage from the last sea battle, leaky seams, or what have you. When they're done, they wait for the next high tide to float the ship and shove it out into deeper water."

"Sounds like a lot of work," Mogi said.

"Oh, it was, no question about that. Nowadays, you put your boat into a dry dock every few years and somebody else cleans it for you."

Mogi sat at a table near a window. On previous days, he'd had to shade his eyes as the morning sun glared off the windows of nearby buildings, but the sky was now overcast. Over Saturday night and Sunday, the hurricane had swung more in the direction of St. John, and in spite of the eye of the storm still being hundreds of miles away, the outer rim of its clouds had moved over the island. The breeze was warm but stiff, setting the harbor's sailboats to rocking back and forth.

Out the window, Mogi's eyes wandered across the expansive harbor as Griffin stood at a whiteboard, giving a rambling lecture on the economy of the New World.

A monstrous cruise ship with ten or twelve passenger decks sat docked at the long pier on the east side of the bay, dwarfing the buildings next to it. It had arrived that morning. After tying up to the pier, maybe three thousand people had burst from the hatchway and into the shopping areas on the other side of the entry gates. A hundred or so taxis, most of which were open-air benches on the back of flatbed trucks, were lined up along the streets, waiting to take people to the downtown area, on various tours, or to activities on other parts of the island.

By late afternoon, the cruise passengers would have rushed back, ready to depart for an overnight travel to their next destination.

Mogi turned his attention back to Griffin. "So, gold and silver were the first things the explorers wanted, then colonization to set up plantations, then sugar, rum, and molasses, and then cotton until the land was exhausted. Then what?

"Don't forget about *black gold*. Slavery started small

at the beginning of the 1500s, first by capturing the natives on the island, then with criminals being exiled from Europe, then indentured servants to work on the plantations, then slaves from Mexico, Central America, and South America, and then captured natives from Africa. The ratio was roughly six to one: six slaves for every white person on the island."

"What's the major money source for the islands now?" Mogi asked.

"Oh, tourism, for sure. We must have three or four million people go through here every year.

"And, unfortunately, the slave trade is still going strong, but this time, it's making slaves out of people by getting them hooked on drugs. In the past two years, the DEA along the U.S. coast has detected a big increase in drug traffic out of Central and South America, and they think it's coming through the Caribbean."

Mogi was surprised. "Why here? I thought the drug trade required a big user community. I don't see that the islands have enough population."

"In this case, it's not a user community the drug lords depend on—it's the ease of smuggling stuff around undetected. They want a place that has a lot of boat traffic going to a lot of different places. I have to believe that it's connected to the cruise business.

"Imagine the amount of luggage that moves between the mainland and the islands and back, plus the cargo that the ships carry. Now, the cruise industry has stepped up and addressed the problems: They only supply ships from their home ports, luggage is scanned or sniffed whenever it goes on a ship or comes off a ship, and they're pretty smart about checking the passengers, too.

"So maybe it's not the big ships at all. Maybe it's the individual sailboats or industrial tankers, even. You can get a lot of drugs into a sailboat. Whatever it is, somebody has figured out a new way of smuggling drugs without anyone finding out how. It's like a cancer in small islands like this one."

"What about Blackbeard's Island?" Mogi asked. "That would be a good source of income. Maybe the islands wouldn't attract the drug trade if more people had jobs."

"That's Padilla's theme park, right?" Griffin asked.

"Yeah," Mogi replied.

"Well, I'd have sunk his ship in the beginning and never approved his buying the land. He must be an idiot if he thinks he can just pick an island and transform it into Disneyland without blowing the whole economy apart. Big numbers of tourists are hard enough on an island the size of St. Thomas, but when you subtract Park land here, St. John doesn't have anywhere near the square miles needed to support stuff like that. So, even if more individuals had jobs, the change in the economy would still be minor compared to the smuggling."

Griffin had crossed to the window, watching the movements in the harbor. "Speak of the devil—there's his fancy supply boat."

In the distance, motoring up to a mooring buoy in the middle of the bay, the fancy catamaran that Mogi had seen on Saturday slowed, hooked onto the buoy, and dropped anchor.

"Just like clockwork," Griffin said. "I can't figure out why they come every day. Why don't they buy supplies for a week at a time? In a few minutes, they'll put a little dingy in the water and motor over to the dock to go shopping at the local fish market. It must be a fancy chef who requires the newest, the bestest, and the freshest every day. Seems like a waste of fuel to me."

Mogi watched as a small boat was let down from the ship and two people climbed on board. It took only a minute for it to get to a small dock where a rope was looped around a pole. The two men stepped up and then pulled a cart loaded with empty boxes behind them as they walked down the dock into town.

"Does seem kind of strange," Mogi said.

"They'll spend an hour loading up their cart with groceries and stuff," Griffin said, "then take it back to the boat, unhook, and go back to East End. Maybe they want to get the mail every day or something. I watch them do it day in, day out. I'd be willing to bet they spend a ton more money on fuel getting here and back than they do on the supplies they buy. I just don't understand how rich people keep any of their money when they make bad decisions like that. Padilla must be an idiot."

CHAPTER 8

There was only a note. After leaving the museum, Mogi had taken the return ferry to Cruz Bay and the resort's shuttle to the Beachcomber. Expecting Jennifer to be off work, he rushed to the cottage but found it empty. A note on his bed explained that she was going parasailing with Adam and would be back by dinner.

Well, shoot!

He wanted to go parasailing and had even told her so.

Why did she go off without him? After listening to Adam's passengers talk about the experience, it was at the top of the list of things he wanted to do. Mogi huffed with disappointment and irritation. It left him the rest of the afternoon to read the history book from Griffin, which he needed to do, but the heat and humidity made it hard to concentrate.

His resentment at being left behind didn't help either.

A little before five o'clock, Jennifer came through the cottage door.

"Nice of you to wait for me," Mogi said.

She laughed. "You have to expect that sometimes our social calendars won't overlap. Besides, you needed to study and I wanted to see Adam again."

"I wanna go next time, okay? It's not like sitting here is my favorite pastime, you know."

"Get over it. I work six hours a day and I'm the reason you're here. Besides, I did a little sleuthing for Glen Parry. Come and look."

Jennifer set her daypack on the bed, took out her camera, and downloaded several pictures onto her laptop.

"Adam came over this afternoon because it was cloudy on St. Thomas. All his afternoon customers canceled, so he took me out instead. As we were riding around in his boat, I came up with the idea of going over to Padilla's place on East End. I had my camera, so when I went up on the tether, I took pictures of the harbor that Padilla uses on the far side of the island.

"First, let me tell you, going up in that parachute is a ton of fun!" she said. "I could see almost the whole island from up there, and Coral Bay is absolutely fabulous from the air! I would love to do it again.

"Second, taking pictures was easy. I was afraid there'd be too much movement, but I think it worked out okay. Let's see what I got." She clicked through a few dozen pictures, each showing portions of Padilla's harbor and the bay around it.

A long wooden dock projected a hundred or so feet into the bay in front of a big warehouse with a large roll-up door and a regular-sized door next to it. Between the front of the warehouse and the dock was a large planked platform where several boxes were stacked. Another building sat about a hundred yards away up on a bluff. A number of people stood or sat in various positions around the warehouse, and the big white supply boat was tied up alongside the dock. Two charter-sized fishing boats were tied up opposite the supply boat.

The rest of the harbor bore the usual rough shoreline and the clear water of the bay shadowed by dark clumps of coral beneath the surface.

Overall, Mogi didn't think Padilla's place appeared much different from what a small harbor might look like, and the pictures certainly didn't reveal any surprises.

Jennifer copied the pictures onto a flash drive and gave it to him. "You can drop this off for Ranger Parry at park headquarters the next time you pass through Cruz Bay."

———

The next morning, Griffin was drawing a rough map of various trade routes when his phone rang.

Mogi's topic for the day was how the different countries of Europe—mainly Spain, Portugal, France, England, and Holland—had fought over various shipping routes around the world, not only in and around the Caribbean, but also the Horn of Africa, India, and Indonesia. Everything, he learned, depended on who was at war with whom at any particular time.

Once they discussed the standard routes, Griffin would show how and where piracy developed, how the pirates operated, where the major pirate hideouts were located, what politics were involved, and why the pirates were eventually driven out of business.

"You seen Adam Deschamp today?" Griffin called to Mogi, holding the phone to his chest.

"Adam? No," Mogi replied.

"Did your sister have anything scheduled with him?"

"No. She's working today, as far as I know. She went out with him yesterday to parasail, and he dropped her off about five. What's wrong?"

Griffin continued to talk into his hand, said good-bye, and slipped his phone back into his pocket. He turned to Mogi.

"Looks like Adam's missing."

CHAPTER 9

It was Tuesday afternoon. Mogi had returned to St. John about one o'clock, having finished creating a trade-routes map with Griffin and eaten lunch along the wharf before he caught the noon ferry. The light rain that began as he boarded the ferry had increased enough to discourage him from hitchhiking back to the resort, leaving him standing around in Cruz Bay for another hour, waiting for the island bus. It was the one thing that he didn't like about the island culture: Clocks and timetables were non-existent.

Finally, back at the resort, it was as he turned off the walkway to Jennifer's cottage that he saw the door was open. He stopped immediately—he and Jennifer *never* left their door open or unlocked. He cautiously entered the cottage. No one was inside, but it was clear that someone had broken in to search for something. Their luggage lay open on the floor, and their clothes had been yanked from the closets and strewn across the beds.

He sprinted up the walkway to the resort office, told them about it, and then found Jennifer in the gift shop.

"They're calling the park rangers since the resort's inside the park boundary," he said as they trotted back to the cabin. Quickly looking through her belongings, it didn't take long for Jennifer to realize what was missing.

"They took my computer and my camera!" she shouted as she stormed around the cabin. "I worked all last summer to buy that computer! That really chaps me," she said, kicking a suitcase across the room.

Glen Parry and another ranger were soon there, looking first at the door latch that had been pried open and then taking pictures of the mess in the rest of the cabin.

"Vandalism is not very common on St. John," Ranger Parry said, "but theft is pretty high. Lots of kids on vacations with too little to keep them entertained. Computers, cameras, tablets, phones—they're easy to conceal, and they all sell well back home. Or, more likely, breaking in and tossing the place was just something to amuse somebody who's bored. Things get worse when rain keeps the kids from going to the beach."

"Well, I hope you catch them," Mogi said.

"Me, too," Jennifer added. "I'd like to find the jerk that did this. I lost all the pictures I've taken since I came here. I emailed some of them, but I didn't think there was a need to back them up. This really sucks!"

"Wait a minute," Mogi suddenly said, "could this be related to Adam going missing? You talked to Jennifer this morning, so everything was still here, which means that it was after talking to her that somebody ransacked this place."

"Oh, I doubt there's any connection," Ranger Parry said. "We talked to your sister about nine, just before she left for work, wondering if she and Adam had been together this morning. If you got here about two, that makes it a five-hour window, which is probably too short for someone to have planned it. This looks more like a theft of opportunity."

The other ranger continued the story. "We got the call about Adam around eight this morning. Adam's dad is a member of the governing board of the Virgin Islands, so he's a pretty big honcho. He lives in the house next to Adam. When he went over for breakfast, he found Adam's bedroom in shambles and Adam nowhere to be found. We thought at first that he had gone to St. Thomas early, but his boat was still at the dock. His dad thought he might have hitched a ride over here to see if your sister wanted to go out in the boat again."

"But why would anybody kidnap Adam?" Mogi asked.

"That's a good question," the ranger replied. "Seems really strange. Adam's pretty well known because of his father, but the Virgin Islands are hardly a place for any political shenanigans that would provoke a kidnapping. And he's as straight as they come—no way he's involved in any criminal activities. It doesn't make any sense that Adam would be a target for anyone."

"Wait a minute. Are you saying that I was the last person to see him?" Jennifer asked.

"It could be," the ranger answered. "But his dropping you off around five leaves the whole evening for him to be around East Bay. We're continuing to ask around, but so far, nobody remembers seeing him. If that's the case, any break-in done this afternoon would be unrelated."

Mogi wasn't satisfied. He couldn't imagine any connections. Unless...

"Wait," he said suddenly. "Maybe there's something else."

He pulled out the USB drive with Jennifer's pictures from the day before. He had forgotten all about it. After he described what she had done, the two rangers grew more interested.

"Are there any computers around that we could view the pictures on?" he asked.

"I don't know about computers, but there's a TV monitor in the restaurant," Mogi said. "They show movies in the evenings. It's a flat screen, so I bet it has a USB port."

They hurried to the restaurant, shielding themselves from the large raindrops as they walked up the steep path.

Once there, the monitor accepted the flash drive and was soon displaying the pictures of the Padilla harbor facilities.

Several resort administrators, including the rental equipment manager, joined the group to view the photos.

After quickly clicking through the images to provide an overview, Jennifer displayed each picture long enough for each to be examined more fully.

Ranger Parry shook his head. "I don't see anything that you wouldn't find on any dock on the island, and the buildings look like standard issue. There's nothing I see that anyone would want to hide. I was right about the lack of construction, though. All those buildings look a few decades old."

"Hold that picture, would you?" the rental manager said. He moved closer to the screen. "Wow. I wish I had his equipment budget."

"What do you mean?"

"See the equipment laid out in a row on the platform? Those are rebreathers, used by divers. Those suckers are five to ten thousand dollars apiece. And they've got the fancy full-face masks with them. That makes for some pretty sophisticated diving."

"What's a rebreather?" Mogi asked.

"A regular scuba diving system, like we rent to you, is based on a diver carrying an air tank with them. They breathe a mixture of air and oxygen directly from the tank. When the tank runs out, they have to surface and get another tank.

"But a rebreather doesn't depend on a big tank. It uses filters to recycle the air a diver breathes out so that he can breathe it back in. There's a small oxygen tank, but it's used very slowly, just enough to make up for the fraction of the oxygen absorbed by the diver. Since you don't rely on a tank, a rebreather system allows you to stay underwater a lot longer. I like them because they don't let out noisy bubbles."

"They don't have bubbles?" Jennifer asked.

"Nope. Pretty slick systems. A regular dive tank runs you in the hundreds, but rebreathers are in the thousands. I wish I had that kind of money."

"Okay," Ranger Parry said. "We've done all that we can do here. Let us know if anything else happens."

"And you'll let us know about Adam?" Jennifer asked.

"You bet. We'll call the resort office and get word to you."

───────

"I thought you were going to the movie," Mogi said as Jennifer came through the cottage door, closing it quickly as the gusts of water-filled wind attempted to slam the door back. The door and windows had been covered on the outside with heavy storm curtains. Dusk usually made the cottage dark, but it already seemed like night inside. The few cottage lamps were small, making the inside of the cottage cozy but dim. The ceiling fan had been running all evening, fighting the still air created by the covered windows.

"It was an old one, and I couldn't get interested," she replied.

"You worried about Adam?"

"Oh, yeah, big time." She plopped down on her bed.

"He's such a nice guy. I don't know why anything like this would happen to him. I'm frustrated that we don't know anything, and more frustrated that we can't do anything."

"Me, too. It doesn't make sense. Somebody stealing your stuff doesn't make sense, either. I bet that ninety percent of the visitors to this island bring a laptop or tablet with them, including the kids. I'm sure Ranger Parry knows about robberies and stuff, but to have your room broken into on the same day that Adam goes missing just can't be a coincidence. Especially since the two of you were together the day before."

"But how could it be connected? The only thing we did was go parasailing. How would that be threatening to anybody?"

Mogi got off his bed and moved to the table, drawing up two chairs. He reached into his daypack. "Let me show you something."

"Oh, your tablet. You're lucky it wasn't stolen."

"Yeah. It was in my daypack from the morning I spent over in Charlotte Amalie. I always take my tablet with me to make notes or take pictures of the drawings that Griffin puts on the board. After you left for the movie, I used it to look at your Padilla pictures."

Mogi arranged some books behind his tablet to hold it at an angle that they could both see and started with the first clear picture of the dock area.

"Okay. This is the first picture that has a good

view of the platform next to the dock. Look at the piles of diving gear. Remember what the rental manager said? Those are rebreathers, very expensive diving equipment. I count eight of them, all arranged in a row."

Because Jennifer had been in the air being pulled by the boat, each of the pictures showed the dock from a slightly different point of view. After ten pictures of moving past the dock— going away from it—the next thirteen were taken after Adam had turned the boat around and was pulling Jennifer in the opposite direction—coming back toward the dock. In each picture, the wooden platform in front of the warehouse was plainly visible.

Mogi pressed the forward key for the next picture and again for the next. After cycling through all the photos, he looked at Jennifer.

"Now I'll go through them again, but watch the platform, the gear, and the people. There's a bunch of guys hurrying to get that diving gear inside the building."

With his progression through the pictures, the sudden appearance of men on the wooden platform was obvious.

Even without having exact timing between their movements, it still seemed that three or four men had suddenly appeared to grab the rebreathers and get them into the warehouse, as if in a hurry. After the last pile of equipment passed through the large door of the warehouse, the door was pulled shut.

"And look at this," Mogi said, cycling again

through the pictures. "There's one guy who is not there, and then is there, and he's looking through binoculars, and he's obviously looking at you. He follows you with the binoculars as you go by.

"Then, there's another guy next to him that wasn't there to begin with, and he's talking into a phone or a radio.

"And look at this. As you're pulling away, another guy comes out of the cabin on the white supply boat and looks up in your direction. I have to believe that you being there and taking pictures got them spooked for some reason. I don't have a clue why, but it's telling us something."

"What?" Jennifer asked.

"Somebody *does* have something to hide. Whatever they think you took a picture of is something they don't want anyone to see. Getting your pictures seems like the only reason someone had for breaking in here and taking your stuff."

"But what could it be? Why would they want to hide their diving gear? It's not like anybody who lives on this island wouldn't know what diving gear looks like."

Mogi leaned back in his chair, crossed his arms, and looked up toward the ceiling. "I don't know," he said. "But there is something going on here. I don't know what it is, but this can't be a random event. Something's up."

CHAPTER 10

"I 'm worried about that boy." Griffin Powers had made himself a cup of coffee and was standing by the window, watching the streets along the harbor as tourists dashed from shop to shop, clutching their umbrellas against the wind in the drenching rain. A cruise ship had arrived an hour earlier, but few passengers had left the ship.

"This is going to keep up for most of the week," Griffin said, talking to the window. "The storm wasn't supposed to come this way at all and is still days out, but we may be in for a bad one. Were you around for Hugo in '89?"

"I wasn't born yet."

"Oh, well, sure. Anyway, there have been some bad hurricanes in years past. They used to be rare in the islands, but I guess global warming or something has made them an almost yearly event. Hugo was the biggest for a while, and then Marilyn came in '95. Damn near wiped the island off the map.

"This one won't be that bad, and they're still saying it will turn north, but even getting close will hurt the place. Once that cruise ship out there leaves, that will be it for a while. Every ship within two hundred miles of here will be heading west." He gave a little laugh.

"Those people who signed up for an eastern Caribbean cruise are going to wake up off the sunny coast of Mexico. The fine print of every cruise contract says that the company can redirect the cruise if the weather forces them. They never cancel. The cruise line isn't about to lose a ship full of paying customers just because of a hurricane.

"Of course, now, the museum will stay open no matter what, so go ahead and keep coming. We've still got a lot to cover."

"Do you think he could have been kidnapped by pirates?" Mogi asked.

"What? Adam? Pirates? You mean like the pirates that I've been telling you about? Oh, I don't think so. There haven't been real pirates around here for years."

"What do you mean, *real pirates?*"

"Well, there are still pirates, even today. For instance, up off the east coast of Africa, there are Somali men in fast boats who go out and use guns to forcibly take over a ship, which are typically oil tankers or container ships. They capture the ship and the crew and take them close to shore, where they demand ransom money for the ship's return. They kidnap people on sailboats, too, but most sailboats have learned to avoid the region. Anyway, it's a bad business that involves thieves who have no honor.

Chances are, somebody ends up getting killed no matter what happens.

"The pirates I've been telling you about are the pirates of history, say two or three hundred years ago. That's who I think of as *real pirates*. They spent most of their time living on ships, sailing around the Caribbean or different places, looking for slower ships that they could run up on and then jump aboard. Most small ships would just surrender and then would be let go as soon as the pirates got what they wanted, but sometimes you'd have the ship-to-ship battles that you see in movies. If the pirates finally took the ship, they loaded the valuable goods onto their own ship, killed the crew, and burned the ship.

"Being a pirate was, in their minds, if not a noble business, then at least a respectable occupation. Real pirates admitted that they were pirates and that they were in the business of pirating, and they expected to profit from the sale of the goods they pirated. Spanish galleons were a big prize to a pirate in the 1600s. In the 1700s, it was sugar, cotton, silk, or rum, which all sold well on the black market. You could make good money if you were a clever enough pirate.

"Of course, most pirates ended up being hung, so they had to be prepared to accept the punishment if they were caught. Most pirates today, including whoever took Adam, expect to end up in court with lawyers protecting them rather than in prison. In my way of thinking, we would do better if we brought back the hangman's noose for those characters. And, while we're at it, hang their lawyers at the same time."

Mogi hadn't really thought pirates were still around, but he recognized that when any ship was out in the middle of the ocean, there were few laws that could keep evil men from doing whatever they wanted. He thought again of Adam: If evil men were on the ocean, they must have counterparts on land, leaving it up to the good people on the land to work against them.

Thankfully, the news about Adam had spread fast. He and his father were well respected, and both were regarded as genuine islanders of the finest sort. That made it harder for the kidnappers to keep Adam hidden or to take him to different places. Hopefully, he would be seen, or at least clues would be discovered. So far, nothing had developed.

"Is there anything we can do?" Mogi asked. "Anything?"

Griffin looked thoughtful. "Well, I do have an observation, but it's going to sound pretty far-fetched. And I'm not sure that it makes any difference because there's nothing we can do about it anyway—it's just an idea. Let's look at those pictures again."

Mogi brought the Padilla pictures up on his tablet as Griffin looked over his shoulder.

"You were pretty clever to notice the rush to get the rebreathers inside, but I can't imagine why they'd care if anybody knew they had the stuff. Padilla is a rich guy—spending a hundred thousand on fancy diving gear is just pocket change. And since this area is one of the finest diving locations in the world, you'd expect him to have lots of diving gear for his guests. And even if the gear weren't for recreational diving, Lord knows that they've got a lot of underwater exploration to do to plan out the piers that the park's big dock will require.

"My observation is about everything else. Bring up that picture that shows a landscape. There, that one. Look at it. See the ruggedness of the place? Most of East End is basically an island, only a tiny land connection to the rest of St. John keeps it from being one. It's got a couple of steep hills, its terrain is rugged, and it's dominated by rocky coastline, my point being that it has almost no roads, no access to the interior, no trails, or anything else to speak of that would get you from one place to another."

Griffin sat back in his chair and took another sip of coffee.

"There's nothing new. After two years, they would have done something—added roads, buildings, something. I've talked it over with Glen Parry, and he thinks along the same lines, though he can't speak about it in public because he's with the Park Service. The buildings haven't been painted in years, the dock looks original, the dirt roads are the same I remember from thirty years ago, there's no satellite dish, no weather tower, no nothing.

"So," he said, stamping around the room as he ranted, "this is where I think differently from Glen. He thinks that Padilla is doing nothing until he gets all the approvals, then he'll turn around and sell the whole property. You know what I think?"

Mogi wasn't sure if it was a real question or not, so he just raised his eyebrows like he wanted to know.

"I think that Padilla wants to stay tied up in the courts so it looks like he can't do anything while he actually is doing something."

"I don't understand," Mogi said. "What something would he be doing?"

"Ah, now that's the question! Did you count the number of people in the picture? Did you notice how many there were? I got at least ten—different clothes, different hair, different looks. There are probably more because who knows how many people are inside that fancy supply boat. That's a fair number of people in a place that doesn't seem to have any work going on. What are they doing? Why are they there? Why all the dive equipment?"

Mogi had noticed the different men but hadn't counted them.

"You counted eight piles of gear. That's at least eight divers. If they were guests of Padilla and were diving for recreation, they'd use the supply boat as their center of operations and all the gear would be on it. The supply boat would be taking them out to the good diving spots. But the dive gear is in a dingy warehouse, so I assume that the divers are not guests. If they're not guests, then they're workers. If they're workers, then those guys are diving for some reason."

Griffin took a sip of his coffee.

"I think they've found a shipwreck. It's got gold and silver, or relics, or maybe jewels from Madagascar or India. Coral Bay used to be the major port in this area of the ocean, and it's where the merchant ships stopped and traded. I'd bet you a dollar that some years ago, Padilla found a shipwreck off the coast, or maybe even in the protected areas, and he doesn't want anybody to know about it so he doesn't have to split the booty with the government. He bought all the land to keep people away from his operations, and now he's taking everything out of the shipwreck without anybody knowing about it. He created this whole Blackbeard's Island thing to cover up the fact that he's *doing* something while everybody thinks he *can't* be doing something.

"It was all secret until Adam and Jennifer came along. My gut feeling is that one of those guys in the photos is a recognized treasure hunter, and that's what they're trying to hide. It wasn't the equipment that was important—it was who was picking it up to hide it.

"Adam grew up here. He has contacts throughout all the Leeward Islands, he knows about the Caribbean, and I bet he would know the guy in the photograph if he had looked. They were afraid he'd recognize the guy, and then everybody would start asking questions. That's why they had to kidnap him.

"But now that they've got him," Griffin continued, "what are they going to do with him? It could be a while if they're diving on a shipwreck, so they'd want him under wraps until then. But if they've found more than one shipwreck, they'd have to come up with something more permanent. I hate to think they might kill him for whatever it is they've got going, but men with no honor may not be concerned about that.

"No matter what, if they're pulling stuff up from a wreck, they'd have to store it until it was taken away. That's what the warehouse is for. I bet whatever is in that warehouse could tell us a lot."

CHAPTER 11

"I tried to talk him into it, but he refused," Mogi said.

"I would think so! It's just a little illegal, besides being dangerous," Jennifer replied.

"But I know that's where Adam is!"

"You don't *know* anything," Jennifer said sternly. "You just want it to be true so you can *do* something. Griffin Powers would be out of his mind to drive you over to Padilla's property in the middle of the night so you could sneak through the jungle and break into the warehouse. Besides, there's no reason at all to think that Adam is inside."

"Look, the only thing that's been different this whole week is that you took pictures of Padilla's operation," Mogi huffed. "According to Ranger Parry, that's never been done before. So, for Padilla's workers, life is ordinary until you show up in a parachute with a camera. Then everybody goes crazy like they have something to hide. If you got pictures of whatever it was, they have to find those pictures and destroy them.

"They know who Adam is, but they don't know who you are. So they take him from his house and force him to tell them who you are and where to find you. Then they break into the cottage to steal your camera and computer. After that, nothing else happens because they think everything is taken care of. They don't know you copied the pictures to a flash drive and gave it to me.

"It *has* to be connected to the dive equipment because it's the only thing that changed across the pictures. So, if they're doing something bad, what could it be? Maybe they're capturing rare fishes to sell to pet stores, or breaking up big chunks of coral, or stealing something else that's protected. Or maybe they're excavating for the piers without a permit. Or maybe they're doing what Griffin thinks—diving on a secret shipwreck because they don't want to pay anything to the government.

"If they'd had ordinary air tanks on that platform, do you think they'd rush around to hide the stuff? No. So whatever they're doing, it's connected to their having rebreathers rather than air tanks. And what do rebreathers do that ordinary dive tanks don't do? They recycle oxygen, they cost a lot more, they don't have bubbles, they…" Mogi trailed off and stared into space.

"Hello?" Jennifer finally said. "Hello? Earth to geek."

Mogi slowly refocused his gaze and looked at his

sister. "The only real difference, other than staying underwater longer, is that divers can do whatever they're doing and not be seen from above. There are no bubbles."

"And this is significant because…"

Mogi shook his head, looking puzzled. "Well, the lack of bubbles ties in with what Griffin thinks. Those guys could be diving on a shipwreck in the middle of Coral Bay and no one would know it because there would be no bubbles coming to the surface."

"I like the bubbles, by the way," Jennifer said.

"Well, okay, but anyway, whether Padilla is waiting for the price of land to go up or is stealing treasure from the government, having Adam is now a problem for him. Maybe they were too quick to kidnap him, or maybe there are even darker secrets that we can't even guess at. No matter what, I'm convinced that Adam is in real danger, and the perfect place to keep him is in that warehouse, so that's where he is."

"So," Jennifer said resolutely, "let's tell the park rangers and have them make an unannounced search of the warehouse. *You* don't have to go there. *You* don't have to break in. *You* don't have to look like a fool if Adam isn't there."

"But *he* rescued *me*! I was going to die out in the middle of the ocean, and he saved me. I owe him. *Me*. Not the rangers, who aren't going to believe what I think anyway. *I*—that's me— *I* need to do whatever I can to get him back."

Jennifer argued, Mogi argued.

"How about if I just take a look?" Mogi finally

proposed. "Look at the picture farthest to the south from the dock. There's a window on the side of the warehouse. No breaking and entering, no encounter with the bad guys, just a look. You run me over to the gate, and we do it at night when nobody can see us. It will be raining, too, so nobody will hear us. It's not that far from the gate, so I'll just take a little hike over to the warehouse and peek in that window.

"If nothing's out of place, we drive back to the cottage and nobody is the wiser. Then we'll know for sure. If there's something going on, I'll take a picture of it and we'll have proof for the rangers. Then they get to do whatever they do. How about it? At least we'll be doing something, and doing something is a lot better than doing nothing."

CHAPTER 12

"I thought you promised we'd just have fun this time," Jennifer said. "This is not fun." The large gate and fence that they had seen on the tour with Ranger Parry loomed in front of them. Another day of Adam still missing had passed before Jennifer convinced herself that something had to be done and that she couldn't let her brother do it alone. The first step had not been hard—renting a Jeep in Cruz Bay with Jennifer's credit card. But now they were actually parked in front of the gate, working hard at convincing themselves to take the second step—getting out of the Jeep.

It was Friday morning, and the hurricane hadn't turned north: It was barreling directly toward the central Caribbean like a freight train. The wind was howling, a constant downpour of rain was beating on the Jeep's fabric top, and not a hint of sunlight could be seen through the clouds. Forecasters scrambled to adjust their weather models, in spite of the poor results so far. They now thought the worst would come on Sunday.

Cruise ships had abandoned the area, moving as far west and south as they could. The Coast Guard had suspended all local boating, and some resorts on St. John were evacuating their guests. The Beach-comber had shuttled their guests into town while workers remained to secure the cottages and build-ings. Eventually, all employees and volunteers would shelter in the park headquarters building or at the Visitor Center in Cruz Bay. The ferry to St. Thomas was running constantly, taking people to shelters in schools and other public buildings.

"We're going to be fine," Mogi said, trying to sound confident. "In and out. We'll go to the ware-house, look in the window, and be back by noon. If something's screwy, we'll tell Ranger Parry, and he'll bring the troops to make a raid."

Mogi used his finger to trace their route on his map of St. John. "Once we get past the gate, Center-line Road continues for another mile, then connects with a dirt road that crosses over to the ocean side of the island to Privateer Bay, where the harbor and warehouse are. It's not more than two miles total. Trust me—we'll be in and out of there in no time. We're just going to look, that's all. Just make sure you don't lose the key to the Jeep."

"It's in my pocket. And what about the dozen or so people in the pictures? Are they going to just ignore two strangers looking around?"

"If there's any chance of being discovered, we'll

come back, okay? We can both run two miles in less than twenty minutes, even in this rain. Once we're back on this side of the gate, they can't touch us, and we'll be on our way to the Cruz Bay shelter."

Looking at each other with determination, they stepped out of their last hold on sanity and left the Jeep on the side of the road.

The first part of the plan went well. Wearing ponchos they had bought from the gift store, they slid around the outside of the fence where it ended at the shore and then walked down Centerline Road, finding it flat and paved until it ended at a turn-around. Moving back and forth to different signs, they found one that pointed to a dirt road that led to Privateer Bay. It was steep going up to a central ridge, something that the map had not indicated. Slogging, slipping, and sloshing their way up, they were soon covered in mud up to their knees. Going down into the bay area was no better.

It was a full hour from when they left the Jeep to when Mogi and Jennifer were crouched behind some bushes on the side of a hill overlooking the Padilla harbor. Despite their ponchos, they were soaked to the skin. Sitting on the ground behind the bushes would have involved sitting in little pools of water, so they stayed hunched over, keeping their arms and legs draped with the plastic, trying to slow their shaking from the cold.

There was no activity in the harbor area that they could see. They'd expected that, but what they hadn't expected was the giant yacht in the middle of the bay

—a huge, sleek, gunmetal gray yacht shaped like a dolphin.

Padilla. It must have been his yacht they had seen several days earlier.

"Oh, great! Now what do we do? We go back, right?" Jennifer said, her wet hair streaming across her face.

Mogi looked around. The white catamaran supply boat was tied at the dock, as were the two charter-type fishing boats he remembered from Jennifer's pictures. The platform in front of the warehouse was empty, and a light beamed out from a window in the building up on the ridge. Floodlights glowed in front of the warehouse and at the beginning and end of the dock, their cones of light filled with waves of blowing rain.

Mogi had hoped the harbor would have been evacuated, but that hope now seemed embarrassingly silly. He had no idea what to do. The yacht was definitely a surprise. If Adam had been hidden someplace around the harbor, he could be found and rescued. But if Adam had been taken on board the yacht, it would take a team of Navy SEALS to break in and search it.

And if Adam was on the yacht, he could be taken anywhere in the world and he'd never be found.

The running lights of the supply ship suddenly lit up, followed by the interior lights, deck lights, and warning lights on the antennae masts. Over the constant noise of the downpour, they heard the deep rumble of an engine.

Up on the ridge, the building's door opened. Several men in slickers held on to their hoods as they left the building and walked down to the dock area. At the same time, the small door of the warehouse opened and two more men stepped outside, joining the others as they all hurriedly shuffled down the dock and onto the deck of the white boat. Two men turned to help with the mooring lines as the others vanished through a hatchway.

The white boat backed slowly away from the dock, reversed, and headed toward the yacht.

In the middle of the bay, the yacht's large exterior lights were turned on, and two men were lowering a long, narrow stairway until it lay outside the railing. Coming alongside, the supply boat rocked and bobbed back and forth as the wind blew it in and out of position, but it was finally tied on and snugged close to the hull. One end of the stairway was lowered until it sat on the deck and then was made secure. A dozen men walked up the stairs to the larger ship and disappeared through a door.

"They probably went on the yacht to wait out the hurricane," Jennifer spoke into her brother's ear. Anchored on both ends, a ship that size, in a protected harbor, would have no trouble handling the extreme weather.

With everyone on the yacht, the harbor now looked unattended, grimly abandoned under a gray shroud of rain.

"Let's go," Mogi said.

It was fewer than a hundred yards from their

hiding place to the warehouse, but it was a messy scramble through mud and rain. Passing the window, Mogi went directly to the corner of the building.

"What are you doing?" Jennifer whispered. "I thought you were just going to look in the window."

"Yeah, well, looking in the window isn't going to tell us enough. We need to get inside."

Staying low, flattening against the side of the building, Mogi cautiously peered around. "It'll be okay—everybody's gone. We won't turn on the light, so nobody will know we're inside."

He quickly stepped up to the small door. Trying the handle, he found it unlocked. Then he and Jennifer, who refused to be left behind, opened the door and quickly slid through.

CHAPTER 13

Mogi's heart was thumping so loudly he thought he could hear it over the rain pounding on the roof.

He pulled the door closed and stood still. The lights were off, but high windows in the front wall let in enough light from the floodlights outside for them to see their surroundings.

There were four interior doors on the left, leading, presumably, to individual rooms. The back of the building held freestanding shelves stacked full of some sort of electronics. A large battery-charging station took up the back right corner, and on the floor to the right were a couple of high-pressure water sprayers, several wheeled carts, tools, ropes, chains, tarps, some boat parts, and other mechanical odds and ends.

The middle of the room was clear except for three odd white things laid out side by side on the floor.

They were about the size of mattress boxes, though half the thickness.

Sweeping their eyes around and seeing no one, Mogi and Jennifer pulled off their ponchos, dropped them beside the door, tiptoed to the center of the floor, and inspected the white objects.

They were thick rubber containers, like envelopes, maybe five feet wide and seven feet long. The rubber walls were stiff, but flexible, and the empty space inside was three or four inches high. One end was open, several thinner strips of hard rubber along each side were obviously made to tuck into each other. On top, several clamps on swivels would seal the container. Around the outside, each container narrowed to a flat edge several inches wide and a half-inch thick.

Mogi touched an edge, finding it stiff and hard. Metal had been embedded within the seam.

Knowing that her brother might puzzle over the containers for minutes, Jennifer pulled on his elbow and they both scampered to the back wall, kneeling behind the shelves to hide themselves, trying to slow their breathing and stop the waves of fear that had sent their stomachs into somersaults. They held still for a few minutes, hearing only the wind and rain beating against the building.

Mogi looked at the shelf in front of him. Across two levels of the shelves were foot-long, two-inch-square rectangular pieces of hard plastic with metal connectors on one end. He picked one up, it was heavy and solid, and the connectors looked like flat plates—it had to be some kind of battery. Glancing back into the corner, he decided that this was what the charging station was for.

"Now what?" Jennifer whispered. "I don't see anything from a shipwreck, and nothing looks like construction equipment. Are we done? Can we leave? I think we ought to leave."

"We have to look for Adam," Mogi said. "If he's here, he'll be in a locked room or something. Stay behind me and watch my back."

They went to each door, approaching silently, listening, twisting the door handles as quietly as they could, opening each only enough to see inside. Two of the rooms were sleeping places: cots, lockers, suit-cases, bags, clothing on hangers. The third room held diving gear: wet suits, flippers, helmets, and rebreathers like they'd seen in the pictures, plus knives, belts, and other things.

The first door from the front of the warehouse was more office-like, with tables and chairs. In the back of the room was another door. It had a large locking clasp above the handle, with a steel pin pushed through the lock's opening.

"That's it," Mogi whispered. The two slipped through the doorway to the back of the room.

Jennifer took a breath and quietly knocked.

There was a rustle from the other side, a groan, and an awful-sounding voice. "What you want?"

"Adam!" she cried in a loud whisper. Mogi quickly slid the pin out and opened the door.

The room was lighted by an overhead fixture.

They could see that Adam's face was swollen and the skin around his eyes discolored. He had a sheen of sweat on his face. He held himself stiffly against a table but managed to grin as he recognized Jennifer and Mogi. He greeted the two with hugs. "What are you doing? You crazy?"

"Probably," Mogi responded with a smile.

"Who else is with you?" Adam asked.

"Nobody. Just us. We've got a Jeep over by the gate."

"Mon, you are brave and foolish," he said with a touch of dread. "Dese men, dey'll kill us all."

"Then we'd better get out of here," Jennifer said in a low voice as they moved toward the door.

"Leaving so soon?" a voice said from the outer room.

They were all startled. Lights blinked on in the first room, revealing two men near the door. One, obviously a workman in a rain slicker, was holding a gun. The other, who was removing his slicker, was dressed in a suit. Who wears a suit during a hurricane?

Oscar Padilla.

"We've operated in total obscurity for two years," the billionaire said, looking at the two Franklins. "Then, in a week, you two suddenly pop up everywhere. First, you go parasailing through my harbor when no one asked you to, then you almost catch us in your cottage, and now, here you are, making your way through a hurricane to rescue a man you hardly know. You two make quite a team, but maybe you should have considered that I'd have remote cameras all over the place."

The soft-spoken man moved to the table and idly propped himself against it, folding his arms as if he were giving a lecture to naughty children.

"But what to do?" he continued. "Adam is too valuable an asset just to dump in the ocean, so we were going to take him to some of our friends in Colombia. He'll do fine there, working in the cocaine business, young strapping fellow that he is.

"You two kids shouldn't feel too responsible about involving him in your escapades, by the way. He was already on my radar as someone who was never going to join my team. He just speaks so well! He's already the one who argues most effectively against my plans for the area which, of course, means that we would have had to address the situation at some time anyway. Your little camera outing just made that day come sooner.

"So, one person going missing was being handled, but now what do I do with three people? That makes it a little more difficult. One person missing could have been an unfortunate accident on his boat when the engine quit and the boat capsized so the body was never found, or maybe a shark has to come into the picture, but two more deaths would cause an uproar and start an investigation that might be a little, uh, uncomfortable for our operations here.

"However, we seem to be in luck. There are always deaths during hurricanes, so we need only to find a way to take advantage of the weather. Your Jeep has potential—a vehicle sliding off a treacherous island road, weakened by the rain. That would work. On the other hand, all hands lost at sea with broken boat pieces washing up on the beach alongside the bodies has a real authentic sound to it. And there are always people being crushed by buildings blown down by gale-force winds.

"What do you think?" the man said in a reasonable-sounding voice. "Anything suit your fancy?"

"You jerk!" Jennifer shouted. "I hope you rot in hell!"

Mogi felt the same way, but his insides were shaking so much that he couldn't make any sounds come out of his mouth.

Adam remained silent, holding on to the doorway.

"Well, I'll let you think about it. You came at an inconvenient time, we were just sitting down to lunch, and my guests would consider it impolite if I didn't join them. I'll be back, and then we'll come to some sort of decision."

The other man raised his gun and pushed the three back into the room. He pulled the door shut and dropped the pin back into the latch.

CHAPTER 14

Mogi plunged his hands into the pockets of his shorts, trying to hide his shaking hands, but found that he was quivering all over. His stomach was queasy, and he could taste the bile bubbling up into his throat.

He leaned into a wall, pressing his forehead hard against the surface.

Everything had gone wrong. How could he have been so stupid to come here? Why did he have to involve Jennifer in his stupid plan? Why hadn't he left it to the park rangers?

Why didn't he think of all the bad things that could happen instead of thinking only about what he wanted to happen?

Stupid.

The light from the fixture in the center of the room was joined by a dim light that shone through a set of barred windows high in the outside wall. Even through the bars, the rain slapped against the glass and the wind howled.

Adam carefully lowered himself to the cot against the back wall of the room. Mogi hadn't noticed the cloth wrapped around his right foot.

"What happened?" he asked as Jennifer knelt on the floor beside Adam and lifted his leg.

"When I first woke up, mon," Adam said, "I didn't know where I was, so I tried to escape. I tried to break de door down with my foot, but I broke my foot instead."

Jennifer gasped as she unwrapped the primitive bandage. Adam's foot was swollen to twice its normal size and was covered with shiny blue blotches from the toes to above the ankle. He had tied his T-shirt around his foot, but had no way to keep it tight.

"What happened to your face?" Jennifer asked.

"Dey wanted to know who you were. Pretty soon, I told them."

"Those animals beat you?" Jennifer asked, gritting her teeth.

"Only a little. I went pretty weak after a while," Adam said.

Jennifer pulled off her T-shirt and handed it to Mogi. "Tear this into strips, please."

Embarrassed by seeing his sister in her bra, Mogi gave her the shirt back and pulled off his own, using his teeth to rip the cotton into strips. Jennifer put her shirt back on and knelt down beside Adam's foot. She used the strips to wrap Adam's shirt securely in place, winding them to apply pressure around his foot. She scanned the room for something to use as a splint but found nothing. That would have to wait.

Continuing to balance his deep breaths against his impulse to throw up, Mogi walked the perimeter of the room.

It kept his mind from thinking about all the bad decisions he had made, not the least of which was leading his sister into danger while also failing to help Adam escape.

Now they were all captives.

The wall with the windows was the same metal as the outside of the building. The other three walls were interior walls with no openings. The door was smooth from top to bottom. Mogi thumped on the door's surface and felt the shallow response of metal. It was steel, which explained why Adam had broken his foot. There was no use trying to force the door open—they could hammer all day and make only dents.

He thumped on the wall next to the door and squeaked out a smile.

"Jennifer, give me the key to the Jeep," he said suddenly.

"What?"

"The key, let me have the key."

She tossed it to him. "Don't leave without us."

Tapping along the wall away from the knob side of the door, Mogi made a scratch on the wall, tapped again for a foot or so, and made another scratch. Between the two scratches, he held the key with its point directly against the wall and worked it back and forth as it chewed away the gypsum of the wallboard. Halfway through, he gave the key a hard pound and it sank to the hilt.

"You don't have to be smart to be a bad guy," Mogi said to his fellow prisoners. "These guys put a steel door in a Sheetrock wall."

It took about five minutes to make a fist-sized circle of small holes. Standing back, Mogi took his fist and rammed it into the middle of the circle. The Sheetrock broke and his fist went through to the space between the walls.

"Ooowwwooooww," he moaned, shaking his fist, opening and closing his fingers. It hurt, but the pain seemed to clear his head and settle his stomach.

Jennifer helped to pull more of the Sheetrock from the wall, creating an opening big enough that they could now repeat the key punching into the Sheetrock from the outside wall.

"What if somebody's out there?" Jennifer asked.

"Nobody's out there," Mogi said. "If they had a guy as big as Adam in here for half a week and didn't worry about him getting out, then I doubt Padilla is worried about us. His ego will keep him eating his lunch, thinking of even more ways to kill us."

Breaking a hole through to the outside of the room, Mogi reached his arm out and around. He pulled the pin from the latch, and the three quickly moved through the door. Straining to be absolutely quiet, they moved to the opposite door. Mogi knelt to the side of the door leading to the large room of the warehouse, telling the others to stay away while he opened it. Cautiously turning the knob and cracking the door open, he glanced around.

The interior lights had been left on. There was no indication that anyone was there.

"He's still got the cameras," Mogi said quietly. "So, once we go out this door, we'll only have as much time to get out of here as it takes one of them to get off the yacht and get over here. Maybe five, ten minutes tops? That will get us out of the light and up the hill."

Jennifer slid her arm around Adam's waist to support him. With a nod, Mogi swung the door open and sprinted to the front door of the warehouse. He pressed his ear against the door and listened carefully for any sound apart from the pounding wind and rain. He looked at their ponchos next to the door and decided to leave them there. Getting wet was the least of their problems.

When Jennifer and Adam caught up with Mogi, she said, "This isn't going to work. We'll never make it to the Jeep. Any other ideas?"

Mogi looked at Adam—he was clearly in pain—and thought for a moment. He cracked the door open a couple of inches and looked at the dock.

"How about borrowing one of those?"

He pointed to the fishing boats tied at the end of the dock.

It was a scramble. Adam hopped as quickly as he could, but it still took Mogi on one side and Jennifer on the other to help him across the platform, down the dock, and into the farthest fishing boat. They expected at any time to see searchlights appear from the yacht and hear a jet ski or another boat start up.

Once Adam and Jennifer were on the boat, Mogi untied the ropes and shoved his foot against the platform, moving the boat away from the dock. The fishing craft was small but had enough room for the three of them to stand inside the cockpit.

"This is where you take over," Mogi said as he helped Adam into the pilot's seat.

Adam found the key in the ignition, looked over the gauges, and then listened as the engine started.

A split-second afterward, a shot rang out from the yacht. Everyone ducked.

Adam shoved the throttle all the way forward and sped toward the sea.

It wasn't until the boat cut through the waves out of Privateer Bay that everyone exhaled, with the harbor behind swallowed in a curtain of rain.

But the difference between being inside the bay and outside the bay almost toppled the boat. Once through the inlet to the open ocean, monstrous waves pounded the small craft without mercy.

"Oh, no! Look!" Jennifer cried a minute later. Through the darkness, the white supply boat emerged, heading to their right, plowing through the waves and coming fast.

By going to their right, the boat blocked them from going to Coral Bay.

Adam made a quick turn of the wheel, curving the boat to the north.

"We can't outrun her!" Adam shouted. "She has big engines. Dey are too fast!"

Now facing into the wind, the small boat was violently tossed and turned by the storm waves rushing toward the east end of the island. The rain, the wind, and the waves all joined until the boat sometimes only skimmed the crest of a wave before it dropped with a hard slap into the valley on the other side. Mogi and Jennifer were inside the cabin, their feet in wide stances, barely holding on to whatever they could reach. Adam stood with his good foot planted in front of the wheel, leaning against the pilot's seat, staring through the glass as the windshield was repeatedly drenched by spray off the bow of the boat.

Mogi looked at the white boat chasing them. Even if it was easily fast enough to catch them in steady seas, it was faring no better than they in the storm, being savagely tossed side to side and slowed by the gusting winds.

It was still closer than before, though, so he knew they would eventually be caught.

No longer able to make Coral Bay, Mogi had thought to land the boat close to the Padilla gate, get the Jeep, and brave the road back to Cruz Bay. But the storm now made it impossible to get to shore—they would be pushed into the coral as they neared the beach and never be able to battle the waves if they tried to swim to shore.

Besides, Padilla might have already sent men to the Jeep.

"Can you make it to Leinster Bay?" he yelled to Adam over the storm's roar. If they could make it to the resort, they could steal the golf cart or the resort's Jeep or even the shuttle, if it was still there. Anything with wheels and they'd have an advantage over the men in the white boat.

Adam looked at the gauges, thought for a moment, and nodded his head. "It'll be close, mon, but we'll make de beach okay."

It was a worrisome seven minutes, the white boat edging ever closer and the fishing boat tossed about as if it were in a washing machine.

"There!" Adam shouted as he turned the boat toward the opening. "I'll head for the right of de bay below de road! Dere's no coral dere, and we'll only be a few hundred yards from de Beachcomber! We'll be all right if we can make it to de beach!"

"Okay!" Mogi shouted.

Adam drove the boat into the large entrance of the bay and headed to the right. The violence of the waves quickly subsided, but the winds still rocked the boat too much for anyone to let go of their handholds. Adam cut the motor just as the boat hit the beach and everyone was thrown to the floor.

Mogi and Jennifer were quickly over the side. Ankle deep in the surf, they helped Adam as he slid over the side onto his undamaged foot. Now struggling through the sand, they looked for the white boat behind them.

It had slowed at the entrance of the bay and was turning back.

"Why are they stopping?" Jennifer shouted.

"Maybe it's the coral," Mogi yelled back, wiping the rain from his face. "They're afraid they'll get pushed into the reef. Or maybe they just gave up."

Adam shook his head. "Dey don't give up. Dey'll do somet'ing different. We need to be careful, mon."

Mogi ran ahead, broke into the storage shed, and returned with the golf cart. It was better than nothing, and Adam was happy to ride instead of hop.

The resort was deserted, and the phone line was already dead. They raided a still-cold refrigerator in the gift shop for drinks and snacks and then piled back into the cart for a rain-drenched ride to Cruz Bay.

CHAPTER 15

The eye of the storm did finally swing north, missing the Virgin Islands by a hundred miles or so, but the heavy rain and high winds continued through Saturday and most of Sunday. Once the storm had passed, the weather quickly returned to bright, hot, and humid.

People were allowed back on the island and into the resorts on Monday, if it was possible. One spot in Centerline Road had caved into a gulley, so traffic was stopped until it could be repaired. There was damage to the Cruz Bay dock, mild flooding in two of the town buildings, and a communication tower had folded in half. Around Coral Bay, two shacks had lost their roofs, and the power was out.

Most people were happy to have escaped with what seemed like minimal damage and disruption, but Mogi Franklin was not one of them.

The ban on boating stayed in effect until Sunday night, making it two whole days before the Park

Service rangers could start an investigation into the activities at Privateer Bay and, in particular, before they could interview Oscar Padilla. This seemed like a violation of common sense to Mogi, and he wore a path into the shelter's floor, angry and impatient over the delay.

Mogi, Jennifer, and Adam had sloshed into town in the late afternoon on Friday, drenched from riding in the open golf cart. The only refuge available was in the basement of the park headquarters building. As Adam was treated by the medics, Mogi and Jennifer rushed upstairs to Glen Parry's office, finding it empty since the rangers were out addressing the many emergencies caused by the storm. Though the news that Adam had been found spread quickly, it wasn't until nine o'clock that night that the three of them told their stories to the chief ranger.

That left the trio hunkered down with other evacuees for another two days and nights, waiting for the storm to pass.

The official investigation began Monday morning with a visit by a park ranger to Padilla's harbor. Mogi assumed that Padilla would have used the time to escape to South America, but the yacht was still anchored in the bay. Oscar Padilla himself led the ranger around the harbor and the warehouse, and even invited him onto the yacht. The ranger was back by noon, and a meeting to review the findings was held later that day in the headquarters' conference room.

Mogi and Jennifer sat at the table, along with Mr.

Deschamp, Adam's father. Adam was at home resting, on doctor's orders. Glen Parry, the investigating ranger, and the chief ranger were ready to start the meeting when Oscar Padilla walked through the door. He accepted the seat next to the chief ranger and smiled at the two young people, who stared at him with open mouths.

The official report was short: There was clear evidence of an attempted robbery at the Padilla warehouse. There was damage to the facility, and a fishing boat had been stolen. The boat had been found and returned to the harbor. No charges were being filed.

"What?" Mogi exploded.

An inspection of the warehouse showed that the Sheetrock had been broken in an interior wall in an unsuccessful attempt to bypass a locked door and gain access to the room. The room was used for storage. Several metal shelves were filled with regular diving tanks, respirators, and masks, as well as Jeep parts, boat parts, and other equipment. Those items must have been the object of the break-in.

The warehouse's large bay held boat parts, high-pressure washers, a jet ski that was being overhauled, containers of oil and degreaser, and tools and garage equipment. The ranger mentioned the battery charging station in the corner but no shelves with stacks of batteries.

"What about the rubber containers? We saw big rubber containers on the floor," Mogi said as Jennifer tried her best to keep him seated.

"Oh, well, I can speak to those," Mr. Padilla said.

"We're installing solar collectors on the roof of the warehouse. The rubber containers you saw were the empty shipping sleeves that held the collectors. I didn't realize they were an issue, or I wouldn't have sent them back to Puerto Rico on Sunday."

The man looked at the chief ranger. "I could get one back, I guess, if you would like to look at it."

The ranger shook his head. "That won't be necessary."

"But you said you were going to kill us!" Mogi shouted.

Padilla laughed. "No, no, I didn't say that I was going to kill you. I said, let's see, that I was going to stage a car accident in which all of you died, or that I was going to put you all out to sea in a boat wreck, or, oh yeah, I was going to bury you all beneath a building pushed over by the ferocious hurricane."

He laughed more and looked at the chief ranger. "Oh, and let's not forget that I was going to send Adam to Colombia to work in the cocaine business. I swear, you should have seen this kid! He was about pooping his pants!"

Mogi's eyebrows shot up and his jaw dropped. "You were KIDDING?"

"Of course I was kidding," Padilla replied in an even voice. "You thought I was actually going to kill you? Look, you trespassed on my land, broke into my building, and were looking for things to steal out of my storeroom. Probably the diving gear. You think you can do that without consequences?

"I'd put you back in that room and leave you for a

month if I could. Obviously, overnight wouldn't be enough for you. I was going to turn you in at park headquarters the next day, but you decided to vandalize the room, steal a rather expensive fishing boat, and then wreck it on a beach. It's only by Ranger Parry's grace that I'm not having you locked up."

Mogi and Jennifer stared in disbelief.

"What about kidnapping Adam? What about his being beat up?" Mogi said in a weak voice.

"I have no idea what kind of adventures you had before you got into my storeroom, but if he breaks his foot committing burglary, it sounds to me like he should find a different line of work."

There was an awkward lull as the investigating ranger continued with the report.

"What about the divers? The equipment? The implication of illegal activities?"

"What?" Oscar Padilla replied, looking confused. "What do divers have to do with you breaking into my warehouse? Just for your information, though, since it seems to be an issue in your mind, I have had several people staying at my facilities. They work for a building contractor who built one of my houses in California. In appreciation for their work, I gave them an all-expenses paid diving trip to St. John. They stayed on my yacht when I was there and at the harbor with the supply ship when I wasn't."

The ranger added that he had viewed the diving equipment aboard the supply ship and no irregularities were found.

"I would also like to note that Mr. Padilla invited

the investigating ranger to bring a drug-sniffing dog," Ranger Parry said. "No traces of drugs were found."

"Wait," Mogi suddenly said. "Why did he want a drug dog?"

"Well," Padilla responded innocently, "isn't that what the big worry is these days? That being a billionaire means I'm connected to the drug trade? I wanted to show that I'm transparent in my business operations, that I have nothing to hide, and that there have been absolutely no drugs at my facilities. I'm here to build a theme park that will benefit everybody, and that's all I'm doing." He shrugged his shoulders.

End of report.

Ranger Parry and the chief ranger thanked Mr. Padilla for coming, and the billionaire walked out of the room with a casual smile.

Ranger Parry stood and faced Mogi and Jennifer.

"It's only because he got his fishing boat back undamaged that he's not pressing charges. Now, I will deal with Adam later to understand what happened with him and his foot. But for the two of you," he said sternly, "you both need to get a grip on your imaginations, go back to work, enjoy your little vacation, and then GO HOME!

"And you," he pointed his finger at Jennifer, "you need to do a better job of controlling your little brother."

Tuesday was a mess. Centerline Road was closed until the road was repaired, and the North Shore road was clogged with people trying to get back to the beaches.

No restaurants had reopened, so Mogi and Jennifer ate the packaged sandwiches the shelter had provided.

It was late Tuesday evening before they were able to return to their cottage.

When they did and when they were finally alone, Mogi went off like a rocket. He was angry, deep down, unmistakably, shaking-in-his-sandals angry. He had made a mistake. In fact, he had made several, and he regretted every one of them, but why were people so willing to overlook that he and Jennifer had saved Adam? That they had found him, beaten and broken, and gotten him out of a dangerous situation? Why didn't they talk about that?

Why did they take the word of a rich jerk?

But, oh no, they were more worried that Mogi and Jennifer had trespassed on private property, and that they had stolen a boat, and that...

Mogi was angry.

Pacing the floor of the cottage and trying to keep his voice low, he ranted and raved and waved his hands and spilled his guts and made long speeches about injustice and the lack of respect and rehearsed what he would say to his mom and dad, and to Griffin.

In general, he vented like a birthing volcano.

Jennifer said nothing. She sat at the end of her bed, staring out the window.

Mogi finally exhausted himself and sat down, embarrassed, on his bed. Getting nothing from Jennifer, he knew that he had fundamentally messed up. Whether it was that she had failed him or that he had failed her, there was now a wall of embarrassment and remorse between them.

"I'm going for a walk," he finally said and, with no response from his sister, left the cottage.

He walked the Leinster Bay road down from the resort and was soon on the beach where they had had so much fun diving on the shipwreck. The partial moon lit enough of the white sand to give him a clear path down the beach. He walked, then jogged, and finally ran as hard as he could, pounding his feet into the sand as if he wanted to punish the beach for holding him up.

He ran and ran and ran until he stumbled and fell onto the sand, shoving his fists into it, crying, then sobbing, and rolling back and forth in helplessness.

CHAPTER 16

"Well, you got Adam back, and that was no small trick. You need to keep that in mind." It was the next morning, Wednesday. Mogi had risen before Jennifer, gotten a ride to the ferry, and had time for a couple of donuts before he took his usual place at Griffin's table, next to the window. He felt drained.

He hadn't wanted to talk about what happened, but Griffin was determined to hear the whole story and wouldn't start teaching until he found out. Mogi started talking without much enthusiasm, but then it all gushed out, sounding more like a confession than a description.

"They must have spent a busy day constructing the crime scene," Griffin said. "I like the solar panels part the best. The ranger should have asked to see the panels because I bet there aren't any."

Mogi was not very talkative, so Griffin let him sit and ponder the harbor while his coffee brewed.

"When will the cruise ships return?" Mogi asked.

"Tomorrow, I would think," Griffin said. "The cruise lines hate hurricanes. They mess up everybody's schedules and it costs a lot of additional money if they have to be sailing instead of sitting in a port. So they stay away as long as they have to but swoop back in once everything is back to normal.

"I've never known for sure, but there must be some central office somewhere that keeps up with which cruise ship goes where. If you'll notice, there's only enough parking space at that pier across the way for two big ships. They take up a lot of space, you know. I've seen three here at one time, which is unusual, the third one staying parked outside the harbor and a tender running out to it. You know what a tender is?"

"No."

"A tender, in this situation, is just a small ferry. The big ship anchors offshore and the tender goes back and forth all day long, picking up and delivering people.

"Anyway, the businesses around here don't want more than two cruise ships at a time and actually prefer only one at a time. If there are too many people in any one store, then it feels crowded and people won't buy as much. Statistics show that two cruise ships' worth of people will actually buy less than one cruise ship's worth of people. Ain't that something?

"So, to go back to what I was saying, there must be some way that all these cruise lines know when their ships should visit the various places at any one time.

Take a guess at how many cruise ships are sailing at any one time."

Mogi frowned and shook his head. "Twenty?"

"Hah! On average, every day during the peak season, there are two hundred seventy-three cruise ships sailing around the earth."

"Two hundred seventy-three? Good grief!"

"That number is from a year or two ago, so I might be fudging the argument a little, but I bet that it's still around that number. That's not all around here, of course, but it does give you a perspective on the business. The Caribbean is popular year-round, and I expect there could be fifty or more cruise ships during any particular week. You certainly don't want them all at St. Thomas on the same day, so somebody's got to be keeping up with where they all go."

Mogi tried to multiply some of the numbers but lacked the enthusiasm for an answer. He gave up but was still impressed with how many people would experience the different islands during a summer.

"There must be billions of dollars of stuff being bought and sold."

"No kidding," Griffin said. "Imagine something as simple as the number of credit cards that must be charged every day. And then think that some of the cruise lines run every month of the year."

Mogi was thinking about the number of pennies that must go back and forth when he glanced back to the harbor. "Padilla's supply boat hasn't shown up this morning. Do they ever take a break?"

"Oh, I never see them when there's not a cruise ship."

"Really. Why?"

"I don't know. I've always figured that it was some kind of supply-and-demand deal. The vendors at the local market, at least the ones who have fresh fruits, vegetables, or fish, know that restaurants won't buy as much on days when there's no cruise ship, so they don't bring much stuff to sell. That presumes that people know beforehand when there's going to be a cruise ship, which, again, goes back to my idea that there has to be a central office that has all that information.

"I wish I knew how to find out. I might take a day off if I knew that there weren't going to be any visitors."

———

There was another note on the bed when Mogi got back to the cottage: "Helping in Cruz Bay. Back late."

Mogi wasn't surprised. He was hoping to find Jennifer and have a chance to smooth things over. She had been really embarrassed and probably felt that Ranger Parry's accusation had been accurate—she was responsible for her brother doing stupid things. She should have prevented all this nonsense in the first place.

Shame that deep might take a while to get over, especially since all the words spoken in the meeting were going to make it back to Adam, which would embarrass her even more. On the other hand, Mogi admitted, it wasn't like he had forgotten the deep-down burn of looking foolish at the rangers' briefing, in spite of the fact that Adam had been rescued. Add that to the anger he still felt at everyone being hood-winked by Padilla, and it was making for a pretty rotten day.

"Hey, Mon!" came a voice from the door.

"Adam!"

Adam had not broken any bones, but he had ripped or over-extended a handful of ligaments from his toes to his ankle. Kicking the steel door had the same effect as whacking his foot with a sledgehammer. He'd be wearing a walking boot for several weeks.

"It's not so bod, mon. Got me a Jeep with automatic, so I'll get around. What are you doin'?"

Mogi took off his daypack and motioned to the bed. "We really could have used you at the meeting last night. I can't believe that Padilla can just lie and lie and lie and everybody believes him. You could have told everybody about being kidnapped and then being beaten up. They would have believed you! They just think I'm an idiot."

Adam laughed. "Don't worry too much. Glen's pretty smart, and he knows not to trust that mon. I told dem all what I know. Now we wait. Dat rich mon is goin' to make a mistake."

They both sat on the bed and extended their legs across the mattress, Adam carefully positioning his walking boot on top of a pillow. Mogi told the islander of his lessons on St. Thomas, describing what he had learned and become fascinated with, and then asked Adam what life was like growing up in the islands.

Adam laughed many times as he told of going to school, singing and dancing in local rituals and ceremonies, snorkeling and diving, being with his father at political meetings, and working an array of jobs that included scavenging the ocean floor for conch, lobster, and historical artifacts.

He had gone to Texas A&M on a basketball scholarship but eventually admitted that he lacked the aggression of the other players. He stayed to get degrees in sociology and math and then returned to the islands to work with his father. His parasailing business was going well, with twenty boats and skippers offering tourists the thrill of a lifetime. His business was centered on the Virgin Islands, but also provided services to a handful of independent islands owned by the cruise lines. He loved the island life—its language, music, and culture—and his business let him help a lot of people across the different islands.

Mogi responded with stories about growing up in the slickrock country of Utah and his different experiences around the Southwest.

"You have de pictures Jennifer take of Padilla's harbor?"

"Oh, sure." It hadn't occurred to him that Adam had never seen them. He unzipped his pack, removed his tablet, powered up, and brought the images to the screen.

Adam took the tablet and Mogi watched as he went through the pictures a couple of times. The third time through, Adam stopped on one shot taken from almost directly over the dock. The camera was pointed down, capturing the dock and the supply ship.

Adam enlarged the image. "Dat's not right. Look here."

Adam pointed at the water beside the dock. It was the typical clear ocean with dark blots of coral beneath, surrounded by webs of sand and sea grass.

"Dat's not de color of sand. And it has straight edges. Dat's not sand."

Mogi looked. Something was in the water about thirty feet from the dock. Whatever it was, it was lighter than the sand and had a straight edge. "Look here," Adam said, pointing to a different place a few feet away. "Nature does not have right angles. Somet'ing is buried in de sand."

He pointed at something resembling a triangle. The inner line was partly covered with sand, but it had two straight lines that met at a corner. Following the line from one side, it disappeared in a shimmer of the surface and then continued as a straight line that met with another straight line, making it look like something rectangular was half buried.

Mogi took the tablet, enlarged the image, looked closer, and then zoomed out. He swished over to another picture. Now that he knew what to look for, several more straight lines and corners appeared in the sand next to the dark splotches. As they looked at the dock and the boats, estimating some gauge of length, they decided that they were looking at six or seven man-made things between the clumps of coral.

Lobster traps? Fish traps? Artificial reefs? Remains from World War II? Foundations for structures? A previous dock? Mooring buoys? Sunken boats? Maybe house panels blown into the bay by a hurricane?

Adam couldn't remember any construction in Privateer Bay and didn't believe that anyone would put in artificial reefs—the island had plenty of natural reefs.

It was a puzzle.

CHAPTER 17

After Adam left, Mogi closed his tablet and slid it into his daypack, still nervous about leaving anything in the cottage. He intended to get a snack at the resort's small grocery store but turned instead down the walkway to Little Maho Bay, where he had his adventure with the windsurfer.

He felt better. Talking to Adam would never have happened if he and Jennifer hadn't found him. In spite of the embarrassment and feeling foolish, getting Adam back was worth what they had done.

His mind, however, was doing somersaults: still feeling the terror of being captured, the storm as they escaped, embarrassing Jennifer, no proof of a crime, the power of being rich, scuba diving and pirates, his parents coming soon, and then back to Utah.

He could imagine the dry heat radiating off the massive rock cliffs at home and he knew he wasn't ready to go back.

Several people were playing in the surf—adults, kids, three or four snorkelers, a man and woman standing on surfboards with long paddles, a couple of windsurfers farther offshore, and in the distance, a large sailboat with full sails, slowly rising and falling in the water as it was toyed with by the ocean swells.

He was amazed. Only days before, a hurricane had smashed through the island, isolating people, driving them from their hotels, homes, and businesses into shelters where they were concerned for their lives. Then—presto!—everything was back to normal, like it hadn't happened at all.

Mogi took a deep breath. He shouldn't be melancholy in a place like this, on a day like this, he thought, but he still felt no enthusiasm for anything.

Finding a piece of isolated beach with a boulder to lean against, he spread his towel across the sand, sat, took his tablet from his pack, brought up his word processor, and wrote himself a letter.

The first days of coming to the island, the newness of the ocean and the air and the smells and the sounds. Loving the small town of Cruz Bay, the resort, Jennifer's cottage, the walkways, and the everywhere-exploding beauty of the island. Excited with his snorkeling, his diving, and laughing at the quaint buildings with thatched roofs and open sides and sandy floors.

He'd be more careful with the windsurfer next time.

He was lucky to find Griffin, the museum, and the park facilities and to make friends with the rangers.

He had done well with his studies, balancing them with his desire for adventure—he hadn't goofed off as much as he could have, and his mother would be more than pleased with his efforts at a hands-on education.

Full sentences were soon too much work, so his letter dissolved into a series of lists.

The history of the Caribbean, including:

1. *Politics, economy, European wars*
2. *Sugar production, rum production, windmill presses*
3. *Ruins in Leinster Bay*
4. *Slavery, triangle of trade, drugs and the slaves of today*
5. *Padilla not doing anything, but looking like he is*
6. *Padilla doing something, but looking like he isn't*
7. *Why the dog?*

Diving on the *Hollander*, which had to be his most fun day:

1. *Blackbeard chasing a Dutch merchant ship, like we were chased*
2. *The crew of the merchant ship grounded on the beach and ran for the hills, like we did*
3. *Someplace, a buried chest full of gold and jewels*
4. *Saw ribs and overall shape*
5. *Beautiful fish, jellyfish, sea urchins, manta rays, barracuda*

6. *The old Danish Road and the stone bridge over the gulley—built in 1718, when Hollander sunk. Did they see it while running up the hill?*

7. *Need to go back to see the anchor*

Everything had happened in two and a half weeks. It didn't seem that long. Not enough time to process what was going on around him, and that, in itself, was something he was learning about the world. People always rush and never see what's in front of them. It takes seeing things, hearing things, remembering things, and thinking about things before you can put all the puzzle pieces together:

1. *Jennifer and Adam's parasailing trip to Privateer Bay*

2. *Rebreathers—stay longer under water, no bubbles*

3. *White bags—thick rubber, metal in the edges*

4. *Adam's holding room—steel door but walls of Sheetrock*

5. *Escape in fishing boat, beaching in the bay*

6. *Driving golf cart back in the hurricane*

7. *Why the dog?*

Griffin had been wrong about the divers working on a shipwreck, he guessed. There had been no artifacts in the warehouse that he could remember, but maybe he just hadn't noticed.

Mogi took a deep breath and closed his eyes. His mother called it a gift. Whatever it was called, his memory was definitely not normal. Maybe not exactly photographic, but he could recall an image—either a page of text, a photograph, or something he had seen, even if for just a moment—and see the details in his mind.

The warehouse. It was corrugated metal, rectangular and tall, maybe two full stories. One regular door next to a big roll-up door, like a garage. The window outside must have been looking into the room with the tables and chairs, the room with Adam in the back.

Standing inside the door, taking off his poncho, what did he see?

Four doors to the left. Heavy-duty open shelving across the back. Batteries on the shelves, foot-sized. Nothing to show what they are for.

A charging station on the right side, like the kind they had at AutoZone, but different—several cables hanging down, a place to set a battery, two cables with handgrip clamps, two or three gauges across the back, batteries, jet-ski size, on a shelf below. Two large high-pressure sprayers, the kind used to wash off driveways or cars or house siding. Other stuff—cans, rags, hoses hanging on the wall, ropes and cables. Windows in the front wall, above the garage-type door.

In the middle of the floor, three white rubber things.

Heavy duty rubber, maybe five feet wide by seven long, maybe three or four inches thick, a sort of clasp on one end. The rubber was thick and reinforced with threads, with tapered sides and wide, flat edges all around. They looked like the padded envelopes you buy at the post office.

Mogi fell asleep, but his mind kept working.

———

When he woke, Mogi rose up from his towel, rubbed his eyes, twisted his back in an effort to relieve the pain, and stretched his neck.

He was starving.

But he now understood why Padilla was so desperate to find the pictures of his harbor and why Blackbeard's Island would never have a single tourist.

CHAPTER 18

t was Thursday morning.

"I need to tell you something," Mogi said as Griffin sat down with his cup of coffee.

Fifteen minutes later, Griffin noticed that he had forgotten to drink it. "This is big stuff," he said to his young student. "When are you going to tell the rangers?"

"Well, there's a problem," Mogi replied. "They think I'm an idiot and a troublemaker. If I walk in with what I've told you, they'll just laugh."

"I don't think they would laugh, but I'm pretty sure that they won't believe you. I'm not sure I believe you. What are you going to do?"

"I don't know. I'm sure I'm right, but I have no proof. Ranger Parry won't listen to me without proof. It wouldn't even do any good to show him Jennifer's picture again."

The two sat for a few moments, Griffin asking for

more details and filling in with some guesses of his own.

He finally stood and walked to the window. Across the harbor, a cruise ship had parked an hour before and was now flooding the landing with thousands of tourists, anxious to get back to the Caribbean vacations that had been so rudely interrupted.

"What time is it?" he asked and then checked his watch. "I have an idea."

———

"I need you to come to Cruz Bay tomorrow," Mogi said.

"I don't think so. Seems like every time you tell me that I have to come with you, I end up looking like a fool. I'd rather work."

Mogi sat on the bed next to Jennifer. "Oh, come on. I haven't been that bad. Sometimes, yes, but not all the time. You have to admit that, right? Sometimes I've made you look pretty good, right?"

"If you've ever made me look good," Jennifer responded, "it was an accident. And this latest incident is big on my scale, even if we did save Adam. I'm not sure I'm ready to let things go."

"Look, I need for you to go with me tomorrow morning to the park headquarters. I'm showing something to Ranger Parry that will earn us his forgiveness. Please? I promise you will not regret it."

Jennifer stared into space, ignoring the pleas of her brother.

"Adam's going to be there," Mogi added.

She blinked her eyes. "Why is he going to be there?"

"He's a major player in all of this, so he needs to hear everything that's being talked about. In fact, he was the one who came up with the biggest clue."

"Okay," she finally said. "If he's there, I'll come. But this had better be good. If it's not, don't be surprised if I ask the rangers to put you in cuffs and throw you in jail for a couple of days."

Mogi smiled. "I'm not worried."

CHAPTER 19

The room was crowded. Mogi, Jennifer, Adam, Griffin, all the rangers. Not a word was spoken until everyone was inside the room and the door securely closed.

Ranger Parry nodded to Mogi, who stood up with his face red and his hands shaking. "Oscar Padilla has a boat that goes to St. Thomas every day to get supplies. It ties up for an hour or two and then returns to Padilla's harbor in Privateer Bay."

The rangers around the room were impatient. There was work to be done. Everyone had heard of the fiasco related to Padilla's supposed kidnapping of Adam and not a few were offended by having to listen to the main idiot involved. Good grief, he was just a kid!

"That supply boat appears whenever a cruise ship is parked at the pier. For the summer months, that's every day. What you don't see is what's happening beneath the water."

He stepped to the side while Ranger Parry turned his laptop toward the group, darkened the room, and played a video.

Mogi pointed. "This video was shot yesterday by putting an underwater video camera on a ten-foot pole and holding it over the side of a rowboat as Griffin rowed back and forth across the harbor, keeping the camera pointed at either the supply boat or the cruise ship. He was able to borrow a camera that had wireless video output, so I used my tablet to watch what the camera was seeing.

"To the right of the screen is where the supply boat is located. To the left is the pier with a cruise ship. The original video had a lot of nothing, so I edited the raw pictures last night. The water's a little murky, as well as deep, so it's dark in places."

The rangers stood and moved closer to the screen.

The video started with a view of the divided hull of the catamaran supply boat. Soon, four divers appeared, one by one, coming out of the craft by an underwater door between the two hulls. Barely visible, a white, rectangular container about the size of a mattress appeared and was held between the divers as they swam downward and disappeared.

The video jumped and now showed the divers coming up out of darkness, appearing next to a much larger hull that was obviously the cruise ship. The divers lifted one side of the container to the hull and then pivoted the rest of the flat bag into place. One of the divers held something against the side of the container and the others let go. The container stayed, becoming almost invisible against the white of the hull.

The divers dropped lower and swam to the other side of the hull. When they next appeared in the video, they were holding another white container. They again went deeper and out of range of the video.

The video picked up again below the supply boat, where the new container was handed through the opening and each diver returned inside.

Every ranger wanted to see it again, and then once more. They did not sit down.

"Oscar Padilla distributes drugs," Mogi said, first clearing his throat, "by putting the drugs inside heavy rubber containers and magnetically attaching them to the hulls of cruise ships while the ships are parked at the dock in St. Thomas. The cruise ships leave, and when they reach some other port, the rubber containers are taken off.

"My sister Jennifer, Adam, and I have seen those containers. They look like big envelopes made of thick rubber, with a really good seal. The outside rims of the containers have some sort of metal embedded in the rubber that becomes an electromagnet when powered by a battery. The batteries are big enough and the magnets powerful enough that the bags can remain on metal hulls for a long time. We saw the batteries in the warehouse in Privateer Bay.

"When the containers are taken back to Padilla's harbor, they are stored in the sand of the bay. We have this picture that shows the containers in the sand."

Ranger Parry stopped the video and brought up

a photo of Padilla's harbor, enlarged it, and pointed out the straight-lined objects on the floor of the bay.

"What he's describing," the ranger interrupted, "is a massive distribution system that could push drugs all over the Americas. Imagine these containers stuck to the hulls of every cruise ship and then taken off whenever the ships dock. They could be put on anywhere and taken off anywhere, in Houston, Miami, Fort Lauderdale, up the East Coast, wherever. The ships' captains would never have a clue that they were moving them. There's no telling how many other facilities Padilla owns that repeat what we saw here.

"I think that we've just discovered the source of the increase in drugs in the last two years."

———

"Okay, genius, how'd you figure it out?"

It was dinnertime, and Mogi and Jennifer were eating pizza at the resort's restaurant. Once the rangers had watched the video and stared at the photograph, it was a non-stop question-and-answer session, with Mogi watching from the sidelines. The implications of what was being done were enormous —every cruise ship, every container ship, even military ships could possibly be used to transport the containers.

Which meant, of course, that absolutely nothing about it could be said to anyone. This was the warning that the chief ranger gave to every person in the room.

If the massive drug-running operation were discovered before arrests could be made, all the facilities would be destroyed, the containers would be deactivated before the ships made port and dropped in the ocean, and the people involved would vanish. The rangers needed time to move as quickly and secretively as possible to inform the DEA and other agencies in the different ports where cruise ships visited. They could only get the whole operation if they captured everything at the same time.

Only Ranger Parry bothered to congratulate and thank Mogi, and then he was off to attend what would be the first of many secret meetings.

Mogi finished his fifth piece of pizza, wiped his mouth, and answered Jennifer's question as simply as he could.

"I should confess that I almost started to believe him. That somebody else had beat up Adam and then locked him in the room and that Padilla didn't know about it. I was thinking that he really was kidding about killing us, that the containers were for solar panels, and that I was completely wrong about everything.

"But I remembered that he lied about the room. It was *not* a storage room, and he knew it. He lied about the building. It was *not* a garage, and he knew it. And he lied about the containers. Nobody would engineer something that heavy and tough just for packaging solar panels.

"But the real breakthrough was when I figured out what he had *not* lied about."

Jennifer looked at him with a puzzled expression.

"Why the dog?" Mogi said. "No one, as far as I know, had said anything about drugs. It wasn't about drugs at all—it was about finding Adam. So why did Padilla ask that a drug-sniffing dog be brought to the harbor? It had to be that he wanted to prove there were absolutely no drugs at his facilities."

"I'm totally confused," Jennifer said. "The dog doesn't find any drugs, so he's not dealing drugs. Why is this a problem?"

Mogi smiled. "Because he *is* dealing drugs. He's dealing a lot of drugs, tons of drugs, all the time, but he's found a way to do it that he believes is absolutely undetectable.

"It's all about ego. The man has an ego bigger than this island, and his ego says that he would love to prove that he can't be caught. He wants the government to do their best to detect what he's doing so he can tell his partners this great story of how he invited the rangers right into the middle of his operations and they didn't suspect a thing. He wants bragging rights."

Jennifer forgot about her pizza. "Wait. He asks the ranger to bring in a drug dog to sniff all over his facility. But if he's dealing drugs, doesn't he worry even the tiniest bit that there might be dust or crystals or a smell or something?"

"In fact," Mogi responded, "his warehouse will not have even the smallest speck of cocaine or heroin or whatever he's shipping. That's the beauty of his oper-ation—he never touches any drugs. He never even sees them.

"The drugs are inserted into the containers at the source of the drugs, like in Colombia or Honduras. The containers are sealed so that they are completely air- and water-tight, and the outside is cleaned so that no evidence of drugs exists. After that, no container is opened until it reaches its final destination.

"In between, Padilla is not involved in distributing drugs—he's only involved in distributing containers. A certain cruise ship comes into port, he takes a container off of it and stores it on the floor of the bay. When the cruise ship with the correct destination shows up in St. Thomas, he takes the container out of the water, puts it into the warehouse, cleans it up, replaces the batteries, and takes it to St. Thomas in the supply ship with a set of divers who, by the way, are using rebreathers so no one sees any bubbles, and they attach it to the hull of that ship.

"If the containers are never opened inside the warehouse, there's no way that any kind of drug would be detected. That's what he said in front of Ranger Parry, and it's the one point on which he was telling the truth."

"But there were open containers at the ware-house," Jennifer interrupted.

"I'm betting that those particular containers were never allowed to carry drugs. Maybe they were stuffed with money. It's as hard to physically move millions of dollars in small bills as it is to move illegal drugs. We just happened to be lucky enough to see them."

"That's pretty impressive reasoning for a geek."

"I may have finally gotten to the truth," Mogi said, "but I am still so very sorry that you were shamed because of me. I am really sorry. You know that I never meant for that to happen."

"I know. But you need to stop thinking it's okay to do something crazy and assume that you can apologize later, like telling me you're only going to look in the window when you know that you intend to search the warehouse. Apologies don't fix the damage that you do along the way."

CHAPTER 20

"I need to tell you something." Griffin snorted into his coffee cup, blowing a spray of coffee onto the table. He mopped up his mouth and chin, then the table, and laughed. "You're a keeper, you know that? The last time you needed to tell me something, you ended up with something so important that we can't even talk about it. I can't wait to hear what you've got now."

Mogi smiled. "My mom and dad are coming tomorrow to spend the week, and then I have to go home."

Griffin shook his head. "Ah, well. I knew it had to happen someday. That's too bad. I'll have to go back to talking to myself. I've enjoyed playing professor with you. You've done good, and I've appreciated you being around. What are you going to do with your parents?"

"Jennifer's going to take a few days off, and we'll tour around the British Virgin Islands and also go to

Puerto Rico, of course. I've told my mom that we're going to teach her to snorkel, but she's not convinced it's for her."

"That will be mighty fine. You bring them by here and I'll give them a good speech on pirates, buried treasure, sword fights, and other stuff."

"And I need to be completely honest," Mogi continued. "I did hold back a tidbit of information from the rangers, but it was because only you would appreciate it."

"Well, my boy, by all means, fill me in. I guarantee you my utmost secrecy."

Griffin leaned over the desk as Mogi motioned him closer and spoke in a low voice.

"There were two high-powered water sprayers in Padilla's warehouse." Mogi pulled away with a smile of victory.

Griffin's face registered confusion. "Okay," he said. "Is that important?"

Mogi leaned over again and continued in his low voice. "I couldn't figure why he had those sprayers. They were obviously not used to clean the floor of the warehouse or clean boats. They might have been used to spray off the platform and deck outside, but why would you have two? If one stopped working, well, you could just wait until you got another one. It's not like the deck has to stay clean all the time.

"But those rubber containers? Those containers, whether they were sitting idle on the ocean floor or were sailing through the water on some ship's hull, were constantly in seawater. And, as you said, anything staying in seawater all the time gets lots of gunk growing on it. Padilla was not only servicing the batteries and making sure the electromagnets were working, but he was cleaning the containers, especially the edges, so they'd fit close to the hulls and nothing would get in the way of the magnets.

"When he was ready to send them along the correct distribution channel, he pulled them out of the water and used the high-pressure water sprayers to *careen* the containers before attaching them to a hull."

Griffin sat back and laughed a good, long laugh, tears running down his face.

"Maybe ol' Padilla is a true pirate after all," he finally said.

It was a few minutes more before they got down to the day's business.

"Okay, so this is our last class, or next to last, if you want to come tomorrow," Griffin began. "I'm here every day, including Sundays. Why don't you ask me questions and I'll see if I can make up some answers? Anything you want to talk about more or something I haven't mentioned?"

Mogi looked thoughtful and then asked, "How big is a captain's chest?"

Griffin laughed again. "You didn't find it, did you? See? There's another reason for you to come back.

"Okay, every seaman had a chest that he'd take with him onboard whatever ship he was serving. It carried everything he needed at sea, and it typically held everything he owned. There was no standard size, but it had to be big enough to hold everything and small enough for him to carry. Inside, he'd put his clothes, knives, papers, money, tobacco, pipes, sometimes craft pieces like pieces of wood to whittle or ivory to carve. There'd be mementos, of course, or souvenirs from different voyages or places he had been. Sometimes flags, handkerchiefs, different hats, and cold weather gear if he wasn't sailing the tropics. We modern-day people can't imagine being limited to a single box for all of our things, but a seaman didn't have much and didn't need much.

"The chests were rectangular so they could be tightly stacked in the holds of a ship. I'd say they were pretty much the size of trunks today, say, two and a half or three feet long, a foot and a half in the other dimensions. Had to be carried by one man, and sailors weren't typically big. Made of wood, of course, but usually reinforced with iron around the sides and edges, and especially the corners, since they got banged around a lot. They had latches and locks, and sometimes a chest would have big straps around the outside, just to make sure it didn't come open. Of course, they all had handles on their ends, usually made of rope."

"Now, a captain's chest was bigger, since he had more clothes and uniforms and such, and also books, writing tablets, log books, charts, and maps. He owned his own sextant, compasses, and other navigational tools. He was also the bank for the ship, so the chest held his personal money, money for the crew's wages, money from selling cargo, and money for buying supplies. There might be a separate strongbox for the money, but that box would be kept inside the captain's chest as well. Woe be it to the crewman who was found messing with the captain's chest."

"So when the *Hollander's* captain ordered that the chest be taken ashore, it was heavy," Mogi said.

"Oh, yeah, heavy on the order of forty to sixty pounds or so. I expect that he threw in whatever he didn't want to lose, so it was probably full. Better make that seventy pounds or so."

"What about gold and jewels?"

"In the *Hollander's* case," Griffin replied, "it's not likely there was much of great value. She was a merchant vessel, bringing goods from Holland, selling them in Africa and Barbados, and then buying stuff to take back to Holland. The captain would have paid a lot of money for the cargo that he was taking back home, so he'd only have enough money left to buy supplies for the voyage. I doubt that any ordinary captain had jewels unless there had been a specific request from one of the owners to get his wife a string of pearls or something."

"Okay," Mogi said. "I was just wondering. Jennifer and I walked over to the Annaberg School area last night, and I started thinking about what it was like on the *Hollander* when she was being chased. You know Jennifer, Adam, and I were chased into the bay by a ship full of pirates. I was scared to death, and I can only imagine what it was like for a crew being chased by Blackbeard."

"He was certainly one of the original terrorists," Griffin said.

"We were sitting next to the old Danish Road, the one from the 1700s. I was trying to reconstruct what it was like—the ship ramming into the beach, men jumping off the ship, running up that old road, struggling with the chest, lugging that thing uphill and hating that it slowed them down so much. I realized that the captain and the crew probably ran from the ship up the nearest trail, which would have been the same road that I was sitting next to since it was so close to the *Hollander* wreck.

"So I went back to the shore and ran up the hill as fast as I could, just to see what it was like. I didn't make it very far, but I made Jennifer laugh, which was good. The hill right there is steep, and if some guys were carrying a heavy chest, I bet they didn't make it but a couple hundred yards before they were exhausted.

"I'm sure they expected the pirates to come after them, so they were still plenty scared as well as exhausted. But when Blackbeard torched the ship and sailed away, I bet they were happy to be alive. When the captain decided to just bury the chest, that was even better news because the men wouldn't have to carry it all the way to Coral Bay. But now the men were going to have to dig a hole.

"St. John is basically a big mountain of volcanic rock, and there's not that much dirt on top of it. So digging a hole big enough to bury the chest would have been a hard job, especially because they didn't have any tools with them. I tried digging a hole with my hands and didn't make more than a few inches.

"That's when I figured out where they had buried the chest. You can go get it, if you're willing to break the law a little. That's my payment to you for being my instructor for three weeks. I wish I could help you go get it, but my parents are coming and I'm out of time. Besides, my mom gets all worked up if I break the law. I'm not sure she'd bail me out if I got arrested."

Griffin slowly lowered his coffee cup, tilted his head, and thought for a minute. "You mean, you know where the chest is buried?"

"Well, within a few feet, but it's illegal to dig it up, so I guess it doesn't matter anyway."

Griffin's face remained puzzled. "You know, kid, sometimes you can be a little scary."

CHAPTER 21

JUNE 15, 1718—LEINSTER BAY, ST. JOHN ISLAND

"Mr. Fleming," the good captain said, "I believe we're on foot from here. We'll make for the settlements, but I would have a barnacle for a brain to think that we should lug the chest with us. Find a proper hiding place to stow it. I'll go ahead to the beach to assemble the crew, find anything that might have floated, and make plans for the night. Tomorrow, we'll strike for Coral Bay. We'll find another ship and come back for the chest."

"Aye, sir,"

Mr. Fleming had been applauding the decision of Captain Teach to leave the bay, though he did grieve at the sight of the *Hollander* burning in the water. It had been a good ship, and he had been her first mate for three years.

But he had heard of whole crews being slaughtered by the madman in command of the *Queen Anne's Revenge*, and he was satisfied that it was the ship and not he that burned below.

"All right, mates, we've got a chest to hide. Look about now."

"We got no shovels, sir, nor even a pick," a crewman said. "And this ground looks hard."

"Cast around for a depression, then, or an uprooted tree. Anything that would give us a start in this jungle."

"By gum, Lieutenant, but there be shovels handy down below where they be putting the span across the gulley, sir."

Mr. Fleming looked down the path, anxious for anything that would aid them in getting the job done. The captain was not one for lollygagging.

"Right! Carlisle, fetch us the shovels and let's be quick to the deck!"

Shovels retrieved, the men searched the area for good ground, yanking and pulling aside vines and leaves and scraping the dirt for some kind of relief from the stone side of the mountain.

"It's no good, sir! We be making nary a mark in this stuff, likes we's sitting on a brick."

Mr. Fleming had watched the men sweating and heaving against the mountain with no progress. It seemed that only the road was ridden of the devilish covering.

The road!

"Aye, look lively, mates. Grab the chest and follow me."

After the arch was finished, the slaves had been forced to carry baskets full of sand, coral and beach rubble up the long path to fill in the space to level the road. The last layer would have been two or three feet of sand, allowing for drainage and making a smooth surface for the bricks.

Once the roadbed was prepared, the bricks from England were being laid out in a pattern, covering almost two-thirds of the surface of the bridge. The putting the final bricks in place had been interrupted by the men running up the path.

"Pull up a few bricks, lads, and try not to mess, we don't want the workers to know what we done."

It took about an hour to move a number of freshly laid bricks from over the span, dig a hole deep enough for the chest, fit it in, fill in the sand, and re-lay the bricks. The men knew the value of hiding, so they took care to re-sand the bricks between their gaps and spread the extra dirt so that nothing looked disturbed. They even smoothed out their footprints.

"The deed is done?" the captain asked as the remainder of his crew gained the beach.

Mr. Fleming explained. "It's a cinch to find, sir. Provided the slaves are no wiser, not a person can discover what we did, and it will be an easy job to pull it out when we come back."

"Good work, Mr. Fleming. We've come out of this a little scathed and the investors back home will be riled, but by gum, we've still got our heads on our shoulders."

CHAPTER 22

PRESENT DAY

The evening sun peaked under the bottom of a cloud that had long dark streaks of rain heading toward the ground, giving it a brilliant gold color that washed the whole valley in a soft glow. The rain would evaporate into the dry desert air before it ever made it to the ground, but the effort was appreciated.

Mogi watched the golden color grow as the sun continued to sink and then watched it lose its brilliance as the sun touched the horizon and disappeared, leaving the clouds with only fringes of color.

Less than a month before, he had been surrounded by ocean. It was already hard to remember what it had felt like, especially as he now looked across a landscape that barely saw water of any kind.

Jennifer was still far away on the island of St. John,

at the Beachcomber, working through her last month. She was also working weekends with a parasailing business in St. Thomas, but it was a minor detail that she did not expand on. She had found a café in town that offered free Wi-Fi, so she communicated with the family through emails.

Tonight was one night of many when Mogi sat quietly, full of lonely feelings and unfulfilled wishes. Coming back had been easy—he'd missed his room, his TV, his internet, his movies, his cool nights. But contentment had not yet returned. He had never been on an island until he stepped off the plane on St. Thomas and had never swum among the brilliantly colored fishes of the sea until he had snorkeled at Little Maho Bay.

He missed not being there. A month of St. John had carved a place in his mind and his heart that wasn't likely to be filled with the slickrock of Utah. It wasn't only the island but the people, the culture, the ocean, and the different way of feeling when he woke in the morning.

His sister, though, was what he missed most.

Their parents had come that Sunday after his last class with Griffin. They were immediately enchanted with the island, the resort, and the sea. They visited, swam, snorkeled, sailed, played tourist, and even went parasailing, thanks to the free sessions Adam gave them. The high point of the visit had been their mother screaming and laughing as she was whisked high above the ocean on the end of a parachute.

It was a week filled with family and many fond memories. But he and his parents had waved goodbye to Jennifer much too soon.

A couple of weeks later, he received an email from Griffin Powers. He was not embarrassed to describe a midnight adventure where he and Adam had dug up *Hollander's* chest. It was in good shape for being buried three hundred years, the road surface of the bridge had protected it and provided excellent drainage. It also helped that Captain Detrich had, at some point, smeared the chest with tar as protection against the ravages of sea travel.

Griffin, being an experienced museum director, assumed the responsibility of opening the chest so that nothing was damaged. *Preservation is everything,* he had written.

Alas, there were only a few handfuls of coins and no jewels.

But what they did find was much better, at least to those who explore ancient times—a tightly bound, well-preserved roll of maps and charts, some current to 1717 and others as old as the late 1600s. The maps provided a more complete view of trade routes, land shapes, settlements, and water depths than what had been known to date.

Along with the maps were tools—cooper's tools, carpentry tools, navigational tools, measuring tools— all thrown in the chest at the last minute and all valuable to any smart captain. Again, more valuable to history than gold.

The crowning find, however, was the *Hollander's*

logbook. With a hasty addition on the last day by the first mate, a Lieutenant Fleming, it described Blackbeard's pursuit of the *Hollander*. The log had been wrapped in oilskin and had survived the years in excellent condition. Among collectors, the logbook itself was worth more than the original ship's cargo.

Among the coins were several gold and silver pieces from a dozen different locations in the New World. There were also various documents, a brace of pistols, clothes that had rotted, and a few mementos of the captain.

After being opened and cataloged, there was a celebration throughout the Virgin Islands for the discovery of a precious glimpse into a world now lost. St. Thomas was planning an exhibition, St. John wanted a permanent display in the museum, and the Park Service, after it pretended to be offended at the law-breakers digging in a national park, staked their claim to an exhibit in the Visitor Center.

There was even an ugly rumor that Ranger Parry had been driving the pickup truck the night of the heist. It was firmly denied.

It all made a good story, and it made Mogi disappointed that he had had to miss it all.

A package arrived the next day. In it was a Spanish gold doubloon, pressed sometime in the seventeenth century, probably in Mexico. Mogi was sure it had been taken from the chest when backs were turned. Griffin himself would have made a good pirate, he knew how to steal with honor.

Mogi smiled as he watched the fading colors of the

sunset. It had been quite an experience. He was already thinking of his sister, how to get back to St. John, and how to find that anchor.

A LOOK AT: RIVER OF GOLD

THE MOGI FRANKLIN MYSTERY SERIES 9

Spending a few weeks in rural New Mexico, Mogi Franklin and his sister, Jennifer, expect a quiet summer of rafting and relaxation. But when they stumble upon an old legend about gold stolen in a long-forgotten stagecoach robbery, their curiosity turns into a high-stakes quest.

The stakes grow even higher when plans for a massive power plant threaten to destroy the serene river valley…and the historic monastery that has called it home for generations. With time running out, the siblings must use every ounce of wit and courage to uncover the treasure, protect the land, and stop a powerful corporation in its tracks. But with corporate sabotage, hidden clues, and even a ghost standing in their way, the journey won't be easy.

The River of Gold is the ninth thrilling installment in the *Mogi Franklin* Mystery series, packed with adventure, environmental themes, and the enduring power of family, logic, and bravery.

AVAILABLE JUNE 2025

ABOUT THE AUTHOR

New Mexico-based **Donald Willerton** is the author of *Death in the Tallgrass*, the winner of the Western Writers of America 2024 SPUR Award for Western Historical Fiction, a finalist in the 2024 American Fiction Awards, and a finalist in the 2024 Storytrade Book Awards. He has written a ten-book Middle Grade/Young Adult mystery series located in the Southwest, two contemporary thrillers, and a fictional World War II adventure novel.

To finance his writing, he used his degrees in physics and computer science as a scientist, manager, and computer specialist, but has always let his curiosity, imagination, and passion for history keep his head aligned with his heart.

www.ingramcontent.com/pod-product-compliance
Lightning Source LLC
Chambersburg PA
CBHW011435170626
46808CB00010B/3170